This book is dedicated to Kim, Victoria, Brett, and all my fans who wanted to know what happened to Millie and Audun.

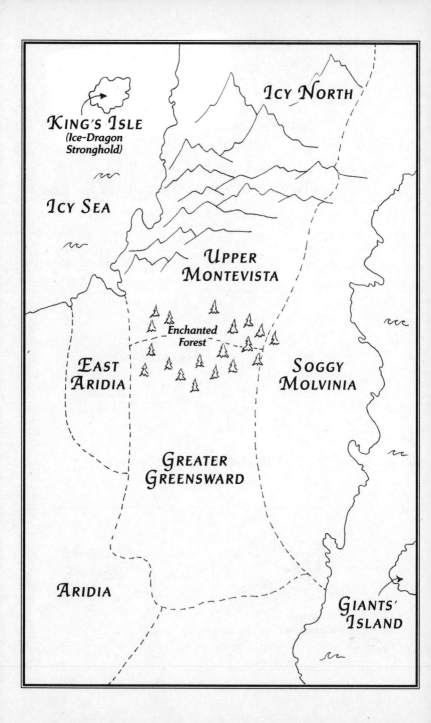

Books by E. D. Baker

THE TALES OF THE FROG PRINCESS:
The Frog Princess
Dragon's Breath
Once Upon a Curse
No Place for Magic
The Salamander Spell
The Dragon Princess
Dragon Kiss
A Prince among Frogs

———

Fairy Wings
Fairy Lies

———

TALES OF THE WIDE-AWAKE PRINCESS:
The Wide-Awake Princess
Unlocking the Spell
The Bravest Princess
Princess in Disguise
Princess between Worlds
The Princess and the Pearl

———

A Question of Magic

———

THE FAIRY-TALE MATCHMAKER:
The Fairy-Tale Matchmaker
The Perfect Match
The Truest Heart

Princess
between
Worlds

E. D. BAKER

BLOOMSBURY
NEW YORK   LONDON   OXFORD   NEW DELHI   SYDNEY

First published in the United States of America in April 2016
by Bloomsbury Children's Books
Paperback edition published in March 2017
www.bloomsbury.com

Bloomsbury is a registered trademark of Bloomsbury Publishing Plc

For information about permission to reproduce selections from this book, write to
Permissions, Bloomsbury Children's Books, 1385 Broadway, New York, New York 10018
Bloomsbury books may be purchased for business or promotional use. For information
on bulk purchases please contact Macmillan Corporate and Premium Sales Department at
specialmarkets@macmillan.com

The Library of Congress has cataloged the hardcover edition as follows:
Baker, E. D.
Princess between worlds : a tale of the wide-awake princess / by E.D. Baker.
pages   cm
Sequel to: Princess in disguise.
Summary: Just as Annie and Liam are busy making plans to travel the world, a witch shows
up and gives them a collection of postcards from the Magic Marketplace. Each postcard
gives Annie and Liam the opportunity to travel to exotic lands and far-flung kingdoms.
What the witch doesn't give them are directions on how to safely return.
ISBN 978-1-61963-847-1 (hardcover) • ISBN 978-1-61963-848-8 (e-book)
[1. Fairy tales. 2. Princesses—Fiction. 3. Magic—Fiction.
4. Characters in literature—Fiction.] I. Title.
PZ8.B173Ps 2016   [Fic]—dc23   2015011955

ISBN 978-1-68119-279-6 (paperback)

Book design by Donna Mark
Typeset by Newgen Knowledge Works (P) Ltd., Chennai, India
Printed and bound in the U.S.A. by Berryville Graphics Inc., Berryville, Virginia
2 4 6 8 10 9 7 5 3 1

All papers used by Bloomsbury Publishing, Inc., are natural, recyclable products
made from wood grown in well-managed forests. The manufacturing processes
conform to the environmental regulations of the country of origin.

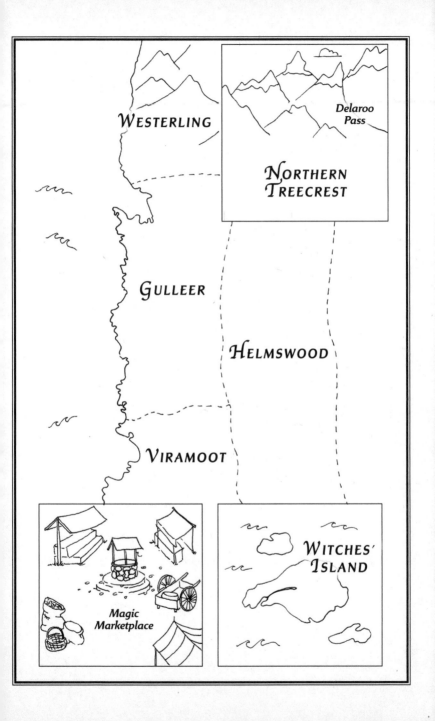

CHAPTER 1

"I HAVE AN idea," Liam said as he spread a map across the table in King Halbert's meeting room. "Instead of going on our grand tour by horse or carriage, let's charter a ship at Kenless and travel down the coast to Scrimsea." After placing paperweights to hold down the corners, he leaned over the map to trace the coastline with his finger.

"I would love to travel by sea!" Annie exclaimed. Although she had glimpsed the large ships from a distance, she had never actually been on one. The thought of sailing on that vast ocean was so exciting! She moved closer to study the small print and irregular coastline, placing her finger beside Liam's. "From Scrimsea we can go to Bellaroost. I've heard that Izbeki is lovely this time of year."

Liam nodded. "Maybe we'll be there for one of their celebrations. I visited Izbeki a few years ago when they were holding a boating festival. It was great fun. They had a sailing contest in the bay and the entire royal family took part."

"Should we stop in Dorinocco after that?" Annie asked.

"I'd be insulted if you didn't," King Montague said from the doorway. Liam's father was the king of Dorinocco and had told Liam many times how much he liked Annie.

"When do you plan to leave?" King Halbert said as he and King Montague came into the room.

"As soon as we can get it all arranged," Liam told his father-in-law.

"And how long do you plan to be gone?" asked King Montague.

"Two or three months," said Liam. "There's so much I want to show Annie."

"There's something I want to tell you before you leave," said his father. "I've decided to hand my crown over to you when you return from your grand tour. I'm old and tired, and with all my ailments, I'm not able to do all that I should. You've proven beyond any doubt how well suited you are for the crown. I think it's time you began your reign."

Annie glanced at Liam. They'd known that he was going to be king of Dorinocco sooner or later, but they'd thought it wouldn't be for many years. For a moment, Liam looked as surprised as she felt. Then he straightened his back, bowed his head to his father, and said, "As you wish, Your Majesty."

King Montague beamed. "You don't know how relieved I am to hear you say that! I thought you might ask me to delay the day, but you've always been one to shoulder responsibility when asked. Very good, my boy! We'll arrange it all when you return from your tour. Now Halbert," he said, turning to Annie's father. "How about that game of chess you've been promising me? I think I'm up to beating you this time!"

As their fathers left the room, Annie noticed how worried Liam looked. Placing her hand on his arm, she said, "Is something bothering you? I'm sure your father is right. You'll make a wonderful king!"

"Nothing's wrong," Liam said with a shrug. "It's just that I'm not sure what I'll do with my mother and brother. I can't leave them locked in the tower indefinitely, but I don't trust them enough to let them out."

After Queen Lenore and Prince Clarence had tried to take over Annie's home kingdom of Treecrest, King Montague had locked his wife in the tower. Prince Clarence had run off to sea, but had returned with the evil wizard Rotan, in yet another attempt against Treecrest. The queen and the prince were now both locked in the tower, and no one wanted to let them out.

"You don't have to make any decisions about them yet," Annie told Liam. "There's still plenty of time to think about it. I'm sure you'll come up with something."

"You're probably right," he said, and patted her hand. "So, back to the map. How far west do you want to travel?"

They were talking about the other kingdoms they'd like to visit when there was a knock on the door and a young page with red hair and freckles peeked into the room. "There's someone to see you, Your Highnesses. I told her to wait in the great hall, but she insists that she has to talk to you right away."

"Who is it, Ewan?" asked Liam.

"She says her name is Holly," said Ewan. "I think she's a witch. Three guards are watching her just in case she's here to do something bad."

"If she's that dangerous, I suppose we should talk to her in the hall, rather than up here," Liam told Annie. "We'll follow you, Ewan. Lead the way!"

The page looked very self-important as he escorted the prince and princess through the corridors of the castle. Liam dismissed him once they reached the hall; the boy looked disappointed when he left.

"I don't think I've ever seen her before," Liam said, spotting the tiny woman seated at a table with three guards standing around her.

"I know I haven't," said Annie.

The woman stood as Annie and Liam crossed the hall. Her gown was made of layers of brown and green, with pockets in every layer. Her hem was short enough to reveal the tips of her shoes and the moss growing on the toes. She wore leaves in her hair, and Annie could smell the scent of pine even before they were close.

"There you are!" the woman sang out, and started toward them until one of the guards blocked her way. Tilting her head to the side, she peered around the guard's broad shoulders. "I came for the wedding, but they tell me I'm a day late. I did so want to see a royal wedding. Or any wedding, actually. I don't get out much."

The guard stepped aside so Annie and Liam could see her, but held up his hand so the woman couldn't walk any closer. Annie was prepared for some kind of witchcraft, but she was startled when a baby squirrel peeked out of the woman's bodice. The woman patted the little head absentmindedly, not noticing the leaf that fluttered from her hair or the cricket that started chirping from the folds of her gown.

"I live in the woods by myself, and few people know I'm even there. My name is Holly," she said, and gave Annie and Liam each a playful wave. "I'm a woods witch and I rarely go anywhere except the local market to sell what I make. Sometimes it's lotions or potions, but I specialize in medicine like tinctures, tonics, and balms. I haven't been more than ten miles from my cottage in years. It's been weeks since I even spoke to another person. Imagine my surprise when I received your invitation! I don't know much about royalty, but I do know that when you're invited to a wedding of any sort, you're supposed to bring a gift. I thought about making something for you, only there wasn't time. Then I remembered all the wonderful things they have at the Magic Marketplace. I was a young girl when I went there last. My great-aunt took me as a birthday treat. The market has grown since I was there, though, and now there's even more to choose from. It took me forever to decide what to get you. Is the wedding really over?"

"I'm afraid so," said Annie. "It took place yesterday. We're sorry you couldn't make it in time."

Holly sighed. "This sort of thing happens to me all too often. I'm terrible at keeping track of the days. Ah well, it can't be helped now. I do appreciate your asking me, though, and I still want to give you your gifts."

"That won't be necessary," Liam told her.

"Of course it is!" said Holly. "I bought them for you, didn't I? Now, where are they?"

Annie and Liam watched as the little witch rummaged around in her many pockets, muttering to herself. Finally she pulled her hand out of one of her deepest pockets and held up a packet of cards. "Here they are! I got you postcards. I thought you might like to see a bit of the world before you settle down, and what better way than with postcards? These should take you to places you've never seen before. I say that because I've never seen them, either. Have fun! Let me know which ones you liked best when you get back."

Suddenly, the little witch was gone, leaving only a few drifting leaves and the smell of pine needles. Although she hadn't been standing near the table when she disappeared, she'd left the postcards squarely in the middle. One of the guards picked them up and inspected them. "They look harmless," he said as he handed them to Liam.

"So did she," said Annie. "Postcards! What a very odd gift! Do you recognize any of the pictures as places you've visited, Liam?"

Liam shook his head as he thumbed through the cards. "It's an unusual assortment, but then, she was a little off herself."

"It was a nice thought," said Annie. "Let's go look at the map again. Do you think we could take a detour to the Southern Isles?"

They were on their way back to the meeting room when the fairy Moonbeam called out to them. Most of the wedding guests had already gone. Annie had seen Moonbeam off herself, so she was surprised to see her back again so soon.

"Oh, good! I was afraid I'd have to flit all over the castle looking for you," said the fairy. "Selbert and I were on our way home when we heard the most awful news! That horrible wizard Rotan escaped from King Dormander before they set sail for Scorios. Rumor has it that Rotan still wants to make an alliance with Clarence, but to do that he has to get rid of you two. My bet is that Rotan thinks if you're no longer in the picture, Clarence will be the next king and he'll make Rotan the royal wizard of Dorinocco. I know you were planning to go on your grand tour soon, but you might have to change your plans. Where were you going?"

"We've been talking about sailing along the coast-line," said Liam.

"Oh, no!" Moonbeam said, looking aghast. "That wouldn't do at all! It would be far too easy for him to arrange an accident if you were out on the water, or at any of your stops along the way. Did you have anything else in mind?"

Annie glanced at Liam and shook her head. "Not really."

"I suppose we could go to one of those places we saw on the postcards," Liam said, reaching into the pocket where he'd tucked them.

"Postcards?" Moonbeam said, her eyes lighting up. "Let me see them."

"A witch named Holly just gave them to us as a belated wedding gift," Liam said, handing them to the fairy. "Some of them look interesting, but they aren't labeled, so I wouldn't know how to find them."

"You wouldn't have to," Moonbeam said after one glance. "These are magic postcards. All you need to do is place your finger on the middle of the card and wish

8

you were there. Oh my! She gave you quite a few! What was her name again?"

"Holly," said Annie. "She said that she's a woods witch."

Moonbeam tapped her finger on her chin. "Hmm. The name isn't familiar, but that doesn't mean anything. I don't know the names of most of the witches in Treecrest. Whoever she is, she gave you a lovely gift and I think you should use it. These cards could take you to some marvelous places that you could never see otherwise, and you would be safe from Rotan. He wouldn't know where to find you! This is your grand tour right here!"

"But they're magic cards," said Annie. "Magic doesn't work around me, remember?"

"Well," said Moonbeam. "That's not entirely true."

"What do you mean?" Annie asked, frowning.

"I gave you the christening gift that kept magic from affecting you, and I'm a fairy. That means that the magic of any fairy or witch won't be able to touch you. But there's another kind of magic that you don't generally see in our part of the world. Dragon magic is the most ancient and most powerful. It can overcome any fairy or witch magic like a shark can overcome a guppy. These postcards were made using dragon magic, which is why they work anywhere in the world."

"Do you mean that a dragon made them?" asked Liam.

"Not at all!" said Moonbeam. "Just someone who used a dragon scale or bit of fang to strengthen it. Whoever it was could have been in an old dragon cave when she made them. That alone would be enough to make the magic stronger."

"Why didn't I hear about this before?" Annie asked with a catch in her voice. The one thing that she had believed about herself her entire life might not be completely true! She couldn't decide if the information was good or bad.

Moonbeam shrugged. "Most people don't know it, and those who do don't want to admit that their magic isn't the most powerful. Besides, it's usually irrelevant in this part of the world. There are no dragons, and very little dragon magic reaches us here."

"I thought there were dragons on the way to the Delaroo Pass," said Annie.

"People call them dragons, but they're really wyverns," Moonbeam told her. "Their magic isn't nearly as strong."

"So you think we should use these postcards?" said Liam. "And all we have to do is touch them?"

Moonbeam nodded. "You have to touch the middle of the card showing the place you want to visit while thinking about how much you want to go there. While you're on your grand tour, I'll find Rotan and lock him away for good. With my fairy friends helping me, we should find him long before you come home."

Liam examined the card on the top of the pile. "We could go to this one first. The views from that mountain are amazing! Look, Annie, the picture looks so real, almost as if you could feel the snow."

"Liam, no!" Annie shouted, grabbing his free hand as he touched the middle of the postcard with the other.

An instant later they were gone, leaving Moonbeam staring at the spot where they'd been standing.

CHAPTER 2

ONE MOMENT ANNIE was standing in the great hall of her parents' castle. The next she was out in the open, with icy winds lashing her with snow and freezing her to the bone. She was still holding Liam's hand, so she knew he was there, but the snow was so heavy that she could barely see him. As the wind whipped the snow into her face, she began to shiver and it only grew worse as she looked around. With the snow coming down so thick and fast, she wasn't able to see much, although she thought there might be a low wall a few feet in front of her.

"Sorry!" Liam shouted over the wind. "I didn't mean to leave yet. We aren't at all ready for this. We don't have money or a change of clothes or anything else we might need."

"Really *warm* clothes would have been good," Annie shouted back, her teeth chattering. "Can we please find somewhere out of the wind to talk about this? My toes are already numb and my ears are so cold, they hurt."

"It's hard to see . . . ," Liam began. "Wait, don't move. I think we're on a castle wall. The edge is just a few feet behind us. That might be a tower to my left. Yes, I think there is. Follow me and don't let go of my hand. Careful, there's ice under this snow."

Annie ducked her head against the wind and took one slow step, then another, following behind Liam. The wind blew over the wall, whipping her long skirt behind her and pushing her toward the edge of the walkway. By the time they reached the tower, her lungs hurt from breathing in the frigid air.

"I think the door is frozen shut!" shouted Liam, yanking on the handle.

Annie moved closer to him, her teeth chattering so violently that she could hear them over the wind.

"Stay right there!" Liam shouted as he let go of her hand. Turning his shoulder to the door, he threw himself against it. On his fourth try, the door flew open and he tumbled into the tower. It was dark inside. Annie couldn't see him until his hand shot out and grabbed hers, pulling her into the small room beside him.

It was almost as difficult to close the door as it had been to open it. This time Annie lent her strength to Liam's. With both of them shoving it with their shoulders, they were finally able to close it, cutting off the wind and snow. Even with the door closed, Annie didn't think it was much warmer inside the tower. It was darker, however, and now Annie couldn't see a thing.

"I saw stairs over this way," said Liam as he took her hand again. Feeling their way along the wall, they found the stairwell and started down, one tentative step at a time. The stairs wound around the tower in a spiral; the small amount of light that came under the door was blocked out when they rounded the first curve. The howling of the wind was still loud enough to make a conversation nearly impossible, so they didn't speak except to say "Ouch!" and "Careful on this step."

Annie had no idea how far they'd gone until Liam announced, "That's the last step. I wish I had a flint with me. Even a spark of light would tell us something." They both started patting the wall with their free hands, hoping to find a door or some sort of opening.

"Listen!" Annie said suddenly. "I think I hear something over the wind."

"Voices!" Liam said after listening for a moment.

They turned toward the sound and spotted light coming from under a door at the same time. The door opened easily, and they found themselves in a torch-lit corridor. Although the light wasn't very bright, it was enough to make Annie blink and squint after the absolute darkness that they had just left. When their eyes had grown accustomed to the light, they saw that the corridor was lined with doors. One of them stood open, letting firelight spill into the corridor. A roar of laughter erupted from the room, drawing Annie and Liam toward it.

When they reached the doorway, they stopped to peer inside. A group of men were seated at a long table, talking and laughing as they helped themselves from platters. Annie thought it smelled like roast mutton, and her mouth began to water. However, it wasn't the food that she found the most appealing, but the heat from the dancing flames in the fireplace. A large, brown bear rug was stretched across the floor in front of the fireplace, and the whole picture was so inviting that she stepped into the room without thinking. The snow on her hair and clothes began to melt away. Water trickled into her eyes, blurring her vision, but it looked to her as if the bear rug stood up and was coming straight at her.

Annie was rubbing the water from her eyes when the beast let out a deep, resounding bark and tackled her, knocking her to the ground. Liam began to shout even as a wet tongue slapped her face, coating her in slobber. A moment later, the men who had been sitting at the table were on their feet with their swords drawn.

"Who are you? How did you get here?" demanded the oldest of the men. Although none of them were wearing any insignia, he had the bearing of an officer and looked as if he was in charge.

"Call off your beast and I'll tell you!" Liam shouted as he tried to drag the animal off Annie.

"Edda, to me!" shouted one of the men. The beast gave Annie's cheek one last lick before backing off, her tail wagging. When she shuffled to the side of a big, burly man with bushy hair, he patted her head and she sat down grinning.

"It's a good thing that was Edda and not Big Boy, or we'd be scraping the girl off the floor!" said a man with a droopy eye.

Liam was helping Annie to her feet when the officer asked again, "Who are you?"

"Tell me where we are first," said Liam.

"This is Delaroo Pass, of course," said the burly man. "Where did you think you were?"

"If this is Delaroo Pass, we're still in Treecrest," Annie told Liam.

The officer scowled. "Still? Where are you from?"

"Treecrest! The castle, actually," said Annie. "I'm Princess Annabelle and this is my husband, Prince Liam of Dorinocco."

"And I'm the king of Floradale," said the man with a droopy eye.

"When were you in Floradale, Delpy?" asked a man with a long, thin face.

The officer turned to the portly man beside him. "Gimlet, weren't you stationed at the castle for a while?"

"Eighteen years ago. When I was there, the king had just married the princess from Floradale."

"That's the problem," said Delpy. "Most of us have been here so long we wouldn't recognize half the people who live in the castle now. What about you, Bascom? You came here just a few years ago."

"I've been here for ten years!" said the burly man. "Yet you all still treat me like I arrived yesterday. And I've never been anywhere near the castle."

"Then you have to prove that you are who you say you are," the officer told Annie and Liam. "Or we'll treat you as we would any spy."

"We've never had a spy here before, have we, Captain Grant?" said Bascom.

"Not yet," said the captain. "But there's always a first time."

The man with the long face shook his head. "We've never had *anyone* here before."

"Why would someone want to spy on Delaroo Fortress?" asked Delpy. "Unless you were a troll, of course."

Captain Grant gave the men an exasperated look before turning back to Annie and Liam. "Prove who you are or I'll toss you out into the snow myself."

"Um," Annie muttered, thinking hard. "My parents are Queen Karolina and King Halbert. My uncle, Rupert, is my father's brother and is in command of this fort, or at least he was last time I heard."

17

Annie glanced at the older man as he sent a black-haired soldier from the room, but she didn't stop talking. "My sister, Gwendolyn, is the most beautiful princess in all the kingdoms, and she recently married her true love, Prince Beldegard of Montrose. She met him when she woke from the curse."

"You mean the curse actually came to pass?" asked Bascom. "How did that happen? I've been here ten years, and I still remember how careful everyone was about spinning wheels. My mother was furious when they carted hers away."

"Queen Lenore snuck one into the castle inside a gift for Gwendolyn on her sixteenth birthday. I was in the room when Gwennie pricked her finger. Magic doesn't work on me, so I stayed awake when everyone else fell asleep. There was no one awake to defend the castle, but magical roses with nasty thorns grew up and no one could get in. I got out of the castle and went looking for the right prince to kiss Gwendolyn and wake her. When I saw that Queen Lenore's men were trying to take over the kingdom, I thought about sending for you men, but there wasn't time."

"We would have come!" cried three or four soldiers. The others nodded and looked upset.

"Isn't Lenore queen of Dorinocco? Didn't you say your husband is from Dorinocco as well?" asked Delpy.

All the men turned threatening looks on Liam; some even reached for their swords again.

"Yes, but Liam helped me!" Annie hurried to say. "He protected me when I went looking for princes and he fought his brother after Gwennie woke up. Neither Liam nor his father were part of Queen Lenore's plan to take over Treecrest."

"We're the last ones to hear anything," complained Bascom.

"What happened after you left the castle?" asked Captain Grant, appearing interested in spite of himself.

"I found princes in the neighboring kingdoms and brought them back. Beldegard was a bear at the time, but it was his kiss that woke Gwennie."

"A bear! You let a bear near a sleeping princess?" said one of the men.

Annie shrugged. "I knew he was an enchanted prince. I hadn't meant for him to kiss her, but it worked out for the best. Beldegard wouldn't have been able to wake her if he hadn't been her true love. They got engaged right away, but before they could get married I had to find the dwarf who had turned Beldegard into a bear and get him to remove the curse."

Annie had moved closer to the table and she took a seat now, turning to face the men when they sat down as well. Edda came to sit beside her, laying her massive head on Annie's lap and gazing up at her with soulful eyes. Annie wasn't sure what to do. Glancing at Bascom, she asked, "May I pet the beast?"

"That's Edda. She just came back from patrol with me and Delpy. And she isn't a beast, Miss, I mean, Your Highness. She's a troll dog."

"I've never heard of a troll dog," said Liam.

"That's because they're all here with us," Bascom said, looking proud. "Prince Rupert has been breeding for them this past twenty years. He wants them big like Edda, although she's small compared to some."

"Just wait until you see Big Boy!" said a man who was Annie's height. "When he stands on his hind feet, he's taller than Bascom there." He pointed at the burly man.

"That he is. Big Boy is one of our best. See Edda's thick coat?" said Bascom as he bent down to pet the dog. "It's got two undercoats. Keeps the dogs warm no matter how cold it is outside, and snags the trolls' talons."

Annie reached out, her hand hovering over the dog's huge head. Her touch was tentative at first, each stroke growing stronger as Edda closed her eyes and relaxed. Petting the animal was soothing somehow, and Annie settled back in the chair, still stroking the thick fur.

"You should hear the dogs when a troll gets close!" said Delpy. "The racket the dogs make is enough to make your hair curl. Trolls stink, but the dogs can smell them long before we can. A troll can't get near this fortress without the dogs telling us it's out there."

"We take them on patrol so the trolls can't surprise us. We're not trying to fight the trolls, just keep them from entering Treecrest through the pass."

"Is this the only way through the mountains?" asked Liam.

Bascom nodded. "The pass isn't bad in the summer, but the snow comes early here and stays late. Even trolls can't get through in winter."

"Go on with your story," said Gimlet. "What happened next?"

Annie cleared her throat and was grateful when Delpy handed her a mug of cider. She took it with her free hand, still petting Edda. After thanking the soldier, Annie took a sip before she continued talking.

"Once he was a man again, Beldegard married Gwennie. A witch tried to kill me at their wedding. I got a message from my friend Princess Snow White that she needed my help. The witch followed us all the way to Helmswood. I confronted her in the courtyard. When she tried to turn me into snail slime, her spell bounced off me and changed her instead."

"Very good!" cried one of the men.

"Excellent!" exclaimed another.

"Did I miss something?" asked a man who had just walked in. Although he was younger than Annie's father, he looked years older with pale skin and dark circles under his eyes. He was thinner as well, and he

21

walked with an unsteady gait, leaning heavily on the enormous dog that shuffled beside him. Annie was certain that this was her uncle, Rupert. She thought that the dog might be Big Boy, because he was one and a half times the size of Edda. The dog's fur was black and white, and his head and paws were massive.

When all of the men stood, Captain Grant stepped forward and said, "The young lady was just telling us about recent events in Treecrest, Your Highness. She claims to be Princess Annabelle. If she isn't the princess, she's good at making up stories."

"When Finlo told me that this girl claimed to be my niece, I looked for the miniatures my brother had sent me a few years ago. Let me see. Yes, here it is. I'd say there is a decided resemblance, although the girl in the picture is much younger."

Annie pushed Edda's head off her lap and stood to peek at the tiny painting. "I believe I was seven years old when that portrait was painted."

"Ah, I see. You're considerably older now. That explains it. Yes, I'd say that this is Princess Annabelle! Please sit down, everyone, and continue eating. I've already eaten in my room, but I would like a cup of that cider. So, what is the news from home?"

Annie noticed that a couple of the men exchanged glances when the prince said that he had eaten. She wondered what that was about as she sat down again. The moment she was seated, Edda's head returned to her lap. Prince Rupert sat across from her, with Big Boy still flanking him.

As most of the men returned to their seats and a few hurried to get cider for the prince and food for Annie and Liam, Annie continued her story. "I was telling them about the witch who tried to turn me into snail slime. After she dissolved in the rain, Liam and I came home. We brought a girl with us who was hiding at Snow White's. The girl was a princess in disguise. When we returned to Treecrest, Liam and I started planning our wedding. The day it was to take place, everything went wrong and a king we'd never heard of before laid siege to the castle."

"How terrible!" said the prince, while the soldiers looked grim.

"We had to postpone our wedding, of course. The unknown king had a wizard with him and he trapped everyone in the castle with his magic. Liam and I were able to get out to search for someone who could help us. We learned that the fairies and witches in the kingdom had been behind everything going wrong on our wedding day. It took a while to straighten that out, and then we had to deal with the king who was still outside the castle. When he left we were finally able to get married. Our wedding was yesterday. Coming here was supposed to be part of our grand tour, but we left earlier than we expected."

"And that brings us to the question I believe we all are thinking," said the prince. "How did you get here?"

"Magic," said Liam, and he gave Annie a meaningful look.

He doesn't want me to mention the postcards, Annie thought. *I wonder why.*

"May I ask a question, Your Highness?" asked Gimlet. When Annie nodded, he went on. "Does a pretty girl named Wanda still work in the castle kitchen?"

"Didn't you say that you were there eighteen years ago? That's a long time to be pining over a girl!" said Bascom.

"Wanda is still there," said Annie. "She's in charge of the pastries and makes the lightest cream puffs you can imagine."

"Ah, cream puffs!" some of the men said, their eyes glazing over.

"There's something I don't understand," said Prince Rupert. "You said that magic brought you here, yet I'd heard that magic can't touch Halbert's younger daughter."

"Most magic," said Annie. "I've recently learned that certain magic can."

"There don't seem to be very many soldiers here," said Liam. "I understand this is a small garrison, but I didn't know it was this small."

"This is the bachelor's dining hall," said the captain. "Some of the men are out on patrol, or working elsewhere in the fortress right now. The men with families share a separate kitchen."

"There are families here?" asked Liam.

"The men are here on six-year rotations," said the captain. "Some leave as soon as their six years are up, but there are others who like it here and want to stay. It's been quieter and more relaxed than most other postings ever since we had the gate reinforced. A few years ago we had a comparatively mild winter, presenting the men with a rare opportunity. A group of them returned to their home villages and brought their wives back here. It was the only time they could go. Usually the trip is long and perilous; no one makes it unless he must. The most difficult part is the route through wyvern territory. Winter is the best time to travel through that region because cold makes the wyverns sluggish, although it also makes traveling that much more difficult. If we try to return to the settled lands any other time of year, it takes at least twenty trained men to make it through."

"The year I came to Delaroo Pass, we lost more than half the men accompanying me," said Prince Rupert.

"That was before we tried traveling in winter," the captain told them.

"I believe we should retire to my chambers," Prince Rupert announced. "I still have a lot to discuss with my niece. Captain Grant, please have one of your men prepare a room for our guests."

"What do you think he wants to talk about?" Annie whispered to Liam as they followed Prince Rupert from the dining hall.

"Lots of things," said Liam. "But I bet magic is at the top of the list."

CHAPTER 3

"YOU OBVIOUSLY DIDN'T want to say anything in front of the men, but you need to explain to me how you got here," said Prince Rupert. "Telling me that it was through magic isn't enough."

"I'll tell you, but I'd prefer you didn't repeat it to anyone else," said Liam. "For all I know, the item may be very rare and valuable. We traveled by postcard."

"What's a postcard?" asked Prince Rupert.

Liam dug the card showing Delaroo Fortress out of his pocket and handed it to the older man. "A witch gave it to us as a wedding present. I touched it too soon and we came here before we were ready."

Prince Rupert held the card close to his face to examine it. "Interesting!" he said, handing it back to Liam. "And you're right. Don't tell anyone about it. That's very valuable and I'm sure people would be eager to steal it from you. If the situation were different, I might have wanted it myself. I assume you have other cards?"

When Liam nodded, Annie's uncle looked thoughtful. "You need to have something you can tell people. Your sudden arrival will spark interest. People are going to be curious about how you got from one place to another. Ah! I know just the thing."

Once again Big Boy shuffled beside Rupert as the prince started walking. Crossing the room, they stopped at a large wooden chest. While the prince rummaged inside, Annie took the time to look around. The room was well lit from oil lamps, some on tables and a few hanging from the ceiling. Two of the walls were covered with cases holding books. A comfortable chair was positioned near the bed; Annie and Liam were seated on two of the three identical chairs placed near a large table in the middle of the room. Tapestries depicting mountain scenes covered the wall on either side of windows that looked out toward the mountain pass.

When Annie turned toward the prince again, he was returning to his seat, holding something in his hand. He seemed to lose his balance when he tried to sit. Big Boy nudged him into the chair and he sat down heavily.

Extending his hand toward Liam, Prince Rupert said, "Here, you can wear this. Act like it's the source of your magic and people will believe it. Then if someone were to steal it, it wouldn't matter."

"Thank you, sir," Liam said, looking surprised. "That's a good idea. I'll make sure I return it after our tour."

Prince Rupert shook his head. "No need. I'm glad I have it to give to you."

Liam slipped the chain over his head and tucked the medallion into his tunic. "May I ask you a question, sir? Why have you stayed here all these years? This seems like a desolate and lonely place."

"I thought so, too, when I first arrived," said Prince Rupert. "Then I discovered just how beautiful it really is and how much I was needed here. Before I came, the trolls attacked every few days, but I found someone to reinforce the gate and now the trolls rarely bother us. This is a peaceful place, for the most part. I've always leaned toward the scholarly side, and here I'm able to pursue my studies as much as I like."

"Your men mentioned that you bred the troll dogs," Annie added.

"That's true," said Rupert. "When I was a young man, I was interested in improving the bloodlines of the horses in the royal stable. There are no horses here, but there were dogs in the fortress when I arrived. I've planned their breeding ever since, and they're becoming bigger and stronger with each generation. Some might find them intimidating because of their size, but they are the kindest and gentlest dogs that you will find anywhere. I see you've noticed my books, Annabelle.

I've written some of them myself. I'm currently work-ing on a treatise about the troll situation. I want the next commander of the fortress to be well informed."

Rupert shifted in his seat and winced as if in discom-fort. Big Boy whimpered and nudged the prince's hand with his head. The prince petted the dog, scratching between his ears. "Now you must excuse me," he said to Annie and Liam. "We retire early for the night here. Once the sun goes down, the temperature drops even more. One of the men will see you to your chamber. I look forward to talking to you both tomorrow. We'll discuss what you might like to do during your visit and how long you plan to stay. Edda will go with you. She seems to like you and I wouldn't want to be the one to separate you. Edda has never favored one person before, but these dogs are known to form very deep and long-lasting attachments."

≈

"This is the guest room," Bascom said as he opened the door. "That's a joke around here. We've never had any guests before. You two are the very first. Breakfast is at sunrise. Be there on time or it might be gone before you show up. Cold air makes big appetites! See you in the morning!"

Annie caught hold of his sleeve before he could walk away. "Wait. Before you go, I need you to answer a question. Is my uncle ill?"

Bascom looked away, no longer able to meet her eyes. "We aren't supposed to talk about it," he said, lowering his voice as he glanced down the corridor toward her uncle's room. "Prince Rupert thinks it's a big secret, but he scarcely eats and he's grown weaker over the last few years. It's obvious that he's in pain sometimes. The only one he's talked to about it is the captain. He must not want his family to know, or he'd have told you, too."

"Do you think I should ask Rupert about it?" Annie asked Liam as they stepped into the room.

"We'll be here for a few days," said Liam. "Let's see if your uncle brings it up first."

Someone had already lit a fire in the fireplace and turned down the covers on the big double bed, but the air in the room was still icy and Annie shivered. Edda pushed past Liam and he shut the door behind them.

"The room isn't bad," said Liam.

There wasn't much space, but there was a tapestry showing mountain peaks and clouds on the wall and a thick rug on the floor. A stool rested by the side of the tall bed, and there was a chair beside a small table in front of the window.

"Actually, it's perfect if you're an ice cube," Annie said, taking off her shoes. "Last one in bed is a frozen egg!"

The blankets themselves were so cold that Annie and Liam had to curl together to try to get warm.

After a few minutes of shivering, Annie was tempted to invite Edda onto the bed for extra warmth, but the bed wasn't big enough for the three of them. Liam fell asleep before Annie did and she lay awake with just her face uncovered. When she was finally warm and pleasantly drowsy, she noticed that the wind had stopped blowing. All she could hear was Liam's breathing and a steady thrum. Annie wondered what was making the sound just moments before she fell asleep.

❧

The first thing Annie thought when she woke the next morning was that something was missing. Glancing at the window, she saw that it was frosted over; light could come in, but she couldn't see out. She was up and getting dressed before she noticed how quiet it was. It sounded odd after the continuous howl of the wind the night before. She was about to say something to Liam, when Edda raised her head from where she was lying by the door and whined. The whine turned into a bark as Edda scrambled to her feet and began pawing at the door. Liam opened the door and the big dog ran out, her bark growing louder and deeper. Other dogs were barking now, and Annie could hear shouting in the corridor.

When Annie and Liam left the room, they nearly collided with Bascom. "Here, put these on," he said, thrusting long fur coats at them. One was the color of cream, while the other was a darker brown. "It's colder today than yesterday and you'd freeze in five minutes without these when you get outside."

The barking was changing as all the dogs in the fortress began to howl. Annie thought it sounded as if they were being tortured, and she understood what Bascom had meant about the sound the day before.

"Do they smell trolls?" she asked, glancing down the corridor where a man was running with an enormous dog on either side.

"That they do," said Bascom. "Your uncle said you can come up on the wall to watch. Bundle up first, though. And pull up your hoods. You'll appreciate them in this cold."

Annie struggled to pull on the coat as she and Liam followed Bascom down the corridor. He led them to a stairwell and they climbed up three flights to the top of the fortress wall. "You couldn't see it yesterday with all the snow, but the wall is twenty feet thick and holds the living quarters. Prince Rupert's rooms and the guest room where you slept are right above the gate. Best view in the fortress, I'd say. Ah, there's your uncle. I should get to my post now. Hear that racket? The trolls must be getting close."

Annie and Liam hurried to where the prince was standing with a group of men. They were all peering down from the wall at the snow-covered pass where dark shapes were shambling closer. Annie looked up, seeing the mountains for the first time. They rose high above the fortress, their sheer walls too steep for even the most nimble mountain goats to climb. Two vertical walls of stone defined the pass; the fortress filled one end of the opening, built flush with both sides so that it was completely blocked.

Annie glanced down. The trolls were much closer now. She was surprised by how quickly they could move. When she heard pounding below her, she guessed that some had already reached the wall.

"The only way through is the gate below us," Prince Rupert said when he saw Annie trying to look over the side of the wall. "I don't understand it. The magic has worked perfectly ever since the spell was cast. The trolls learned how fruitless it was to attack the gate, but they seem to think they can get through now."

"The gate is impenetrable because of magic?" asked Annie. "Someone should have told me! Magic doesn't work around me, remember? And I slept in a room above the gate."

Her uncle frowned, his eyes flicking from the approaching trolls back to Annie. "Do you mean to say that your presence was enough to remove the spell?"

Annie nodded. "It happens all the time. It works faster if I touch something, but even when I'm close by, I make the magic fade. I didn't know there was magic here. I can hear it when it's present, but the wind was so loud last night, it would have drowned out anything else. Come to think of it, I did hear something when the wind stopped. The sound is gone now, but the magic should return when I'm no longer here. The trolls must be able to hear it, too. That's how they know it's gone. Liam and I should leave now, before they break through the gate. Here, we'll give you back your coats."

"No, no, keep them on!" said Prince Rupert. "You'll freeze in an instant if you take them off now. I'm glad I was finally able to meet you, Annie. You, too, Liam. I hope to see you again someday."

"So do I," said Annie as Liam shook her uncle's hand. "Perhaps in warmer circumstances!"

Annie wasn't sure if she should hug Prince Rupert or not; he didn't seem like the hugging sort. She finally decided that she would and gave him a quick kiss on the cheek besides. He seemed surprised and patted her back as if he didn't know what else to do.

"Ready?" Annie said, turning to Liam.

"Here's the next card," he said, holding it in front of her.

"Good-bye!" they called to the prince and the men on the wall. And then they touched the middle of the card and were gone.

CHAPTER 4

"MORE MOUNTAINS?" ANNIE said as she looked around. "At least we're dressed for it this time." She hadn't had a chance to look at the card before she touched it, so she hadn't known what to expect. They had arrived in a courtyard with the white walls of a large palace around them. Tall towers with pointed spires stood at the four corners, and a two-story white stone building took up much of the space. Beyond the courtyard walls, snow-topped mountains rose on every side. The sun was just coming up over one set of peaks, revealing more of the scenery every second.

"If the sun is coming up here, we must be west of Delaroo Pass," said Annie. "Where do you think we are?"

Liam shook his head. "I don't know. I've never seen any place like this before. This is amazing. It looks as if there's snow on the ground outside the walls, but the air is balmy here. I'm hot in this coat. I'm going to take it off."

Annie agreed. She was sweating with the coat on, and the air on her face felt far too warm for there to be snow. Pushing back her hood, she took off her coat and ran her fingers through her hair. She could hear the sound of splashing water now. When she looked for the source, she spotted a stone circle surrounding a fountain where water rose into the air and cascaded down in droplets. The most unusual thing about the fountain was the cloud of mist that hung over it, hiding the water one moment and revealing it the next.

"Why is it warm here when it's so cold just beyond the walls?" Liam wondered aloud.

"It must be magic," Annie said. "But if it is, it won't last long with me here. Look at that fountain. Do you see the cloud above it?"

"That's odd," said Liam. "Do you think the water is warm, too?"

They strode to the fountain with their coats draped over their arms. Annie sat on the stone edging and reached her hand toward the water. She was about to touch it when Liam saw what she was doing and said, "Wait! We don't know if it's safe. Is that steam or mist coming off it?"

Annie pulled her hand back and peered down into the water. It wasn't boiling or anything, but Liam was right; they didn't know what the water vapor meant.

37

They were both standing by the fountain when they heard shouting. Turning to look, they saw a small boy run through an open doorway, laughing. Wearing just an under-tunic, he had the rolling gait of a very young child. He was darting across the courtyard when a young woman dressed in a rich-blue, shapeless gown ran through the same doorway, calling, "Marco!" followed by something in a language that Annie didn't understand.

Catching up with the child, the woman swung him off his feet and twirled him around. Another woman bustled after her, carrying a blanket. Annie had a feeling that the second woman was a servant; although they were both dressed in the same style, the second woman's gown was made from a coarser fabric and she nodded in deference to the younger woman before handing her the blanket.

The young woman was talking to the little boy when he noticed Annie and Liam. He said something to the woman and she turned her head to look at them. Surprised, she pulled the little boy closer to her. When a bearded man came through the doorway a moment later, she called to him, again in the language that Annie didn't understand.

Like the women, the man was wearing a shapeless garment that covered him from neck to feet. The blue fabric was finer than that of the older woman's, and he had the bearing of a man in charge when he started toward Annie and Liam.

Liam moved toward Annie so that he was standing slightly in front of her while touching her arm with his. She noticed that he held one hand near the pocket where he had tucked the postcards, and was holding the medallion with the other.

"We didn't mean to surprise you," Liam said as the man drew close. "My name is Prince Liam, and this is my wife, Princess Annabelle. We've come to visit, but if this isn't a good time, we can leave."

Annie hoped the man could speak the same language, and was relieved when he said, "Welcome to Westerling! You have arrived at a most propitious time. We rarely have visitors during Shumra. Are you here to join us in meditation?"

"Actually, we were just married and are on our grand tour. A friend gave us a magical gift that will take us to far-off lands," Liam said, patting the medallion. "We wanted to visit places that we had never seen before."

"Then you are doubly welcome here," said the man. "You honor us with your presence at such an important point in your lives. I am King Lalidama and this is my wife, Queen Shareeza. The runaway child is our son, Prince Marco."

When the little boy looked up at them with laughing eyes, Annie felt her heart melt.

"You must have powerful magic here, to make the air of your palace so warm when there is snow all around you," said Liam.

"That is not magic, other than the magic that nature gives us. Our palace is built above hot springs that keep us warm no matter how cold the weather. Come. Join us! We were about to break our fast as a family as we do every morning."

Westerling! Annie thought as Liam accepted the invitation. *That's where the mystics live!*

She and Liam had met someone who had claimed to be a prince from Westerling, but was really the adolescent son of a nasty witch. They had later learned that the prince of the far-off land was a two-year-old named Marco. Annie was excited to finally meet him.

As Annie and Liam followed the king and his family into the palace, they couldn't keep from staring. The walls and floors were as white as the snow in the mountains, while the ceiling was covered with blue tiles the color of the sky. Murals depicting scenes from nature had been painted on some of the walls. A glimpse through an open doorway revealed men and women seated cross-legged in a circle, their eyes closed and their faces serene. All were wearing the same shapeless gowns as the king and queen, although the colors varied.

They had been in the palace for only a few minutes when the serving woman whisked the little prince away. No one seemed to react when a large golden-colored cat passed them as it prowled the hallways. It spared them only the briefest of glances before moving on. The cat made her think of Edda, and how comforting it had been to have the dog close by, if only for a little while.

They finally reached a large, open room with windows looking out over the mountains. The tables were low to the floor, and there were no chairs or benches. Instead there were pillows placed on the floor on three sides of the table. A bowl held an arrangement of delicate white and yellow flowers, scenting the air with their perfume. The king and queen waited patiently while a serving woman hurried to bring more pillows for the guests, and other servants brought bowls of fresh fruit, cooked grains rich with spices, and eggs cooked in a milky broth. Cups of sparkling water were set on the table along with clay pitchers dripping with condensation.

Annie and Liam waited for the king and queen to sit, but no one moved toward the table until the serving woman brought the prince to the room, dressed in a garment like his parents'. The king sat first with his wife and son on either side of him. Annie and Liam sat farther down the table. The little boy squirmed until his mother served him grain and eggs. His father didn't seem to notice as Marco devoured the first few bites, then began to play with his food. The queen chided her son, telling him to stop. He did, but began to fidget again.

"Your palace is lovely," Annie said, breaking the silence as everyone helped themselves to the food. "And the view is extraordinary."

"You are most gracious," said the king. "However, we are more interested in the tranquillity of our surroundings than in the outward appearance. The palace was built to encourage meditation."

Marco reached for a piece of egg. It was soft from the milky broth, a texture he seemed to like. He laughed as he squeezed it with his hand, and the egg oozed out between his fingers. Queen Shareeza sighed and wiped his hand clean with a cloth she pulled from the folds of her garment.

"You said that hot springs keep your palace warm," said Annie. "Do you use magic for anything here? The last place we visited was made strong through magic."

The king shook his head. "This is a peaceful kingdom. The mountains are protection enough." He turned to his food and studied it as if he'd never seen anything like it before. Using a shallow spoon, he scooped up a bite of grain and began to eat.

Although Queen Shareeza had food on her own trencher, she was more intent on tending to her son. The little prince was pushing his grain to the sides of his plate, making a mushy wall. The queen looked as if she wanted to say something, but didn't after a quick glance at her husband.

Liam was enjoying his breakfast and didn't notice anything going on around him. The silence lengthened while the king chewed each bite slowly and methodically. Annie was used to lively conservations during a meal. It bothered her that no one was talking. "The flowers are beautiful," she finally said. "Where do you get fresh flowers among all this snow? Do you grow them here at your palace?"

"They came from somewhere out there," the king said, waving his hand toward the window.

For the first time, the queen looked interested. "There is a meadow filled with flowers that grow even in the snow," she said, her eyes lighting up. "You can almost see it from here." She pointed out the window to a narrow pass that widened out farther up the slope. "It is my favorite place to visit when I have the time. I saw a snow owl there once, and I often see rock dodgers."

"What are rock dodgers?" asked Liam.

"They're like rabbits, only bigger and plumper. People in the city in which I grew up prized them for their meat. Which we do not eat here," she said, glancing at her husband.

"Rock dodgers? Interesting," said Liam.

When no one seemed inclined to talk any longer, Annie gave up. She ate the grain and a small fruit that reminded her of a plum, but wasn't interested in the eggs after seeing Marco play with his.

After a while, the little boy began to kick the table. His mother sighed and gestured to a servant hidden behind the door. The woman whisked Marco away, whispering something that managed to quiet the little boy.

Queen Shareeza had just picked up her spoon to start eating, when the king set his on the edge of his trencher and said to Annie and Liam, "You are welcome to stay as long as you would like. However, we won't be able to talk to you again until dusk, when we eat our next meal. Queen Shareeza and I spend most of our day in meditation. You may join us if you'd like, but we won't insist, as you are visitors. If you'd prefer, feel free to explore the palace. All we ask is that you do not disturb anyone who is meditating. Come, my dear. It is time." He held out his hand to his wife, who reluctantly set down her spoon.

Annie had the feeling that the king was the only one who was enthusiastic about meditating. Although she was curious about how they did it, she wasn't interested enough to spend the entire day finding out.

After King Lalidama and Queen Shareeza left the room, Annie and Liam followed them to the door. When the king and queen turned left, Annie and Liam turned right. Walking to the end of the hallway, they set about exploring the palace and were continually surprised when they came across something new and different.

The palace was so unlike anywhere else they'd been that Annie found herself gawking again. In one room they found a pool where red and gold fish swam, swishing their long, plumed tails. The kitchen was down another hallway. It was roomy and had three ovens, each big enough to roast an ox. The cooks were very nice and gave Annie and Liam pieces of flat bread smeared with a crunchy nut spread.

They found a room filled with boots and coats and hats for wearing in the snow. The door beside it led outside. Another door opened into a room filled with racks holding bows and arrows, swords and spears. "An armory!" Liam said. "Why would mystics have weapons like these? I thought the king said that the mountains were all the protection they need."

"I don't know," said Annie. "But don't most people keep the doors to their armory locked?"

"Yes, they do," Liam said, looking puzzled.

Continuing their search, they came across a stairwell leading to the second floor. The railings were carved in delicate swoops and whirls, and the steps themselves were covered in intricate mosaics. When Annie and Liam peeked inside an open door, they saw the little prince sitting on the floor, playing with a young woman. Voices drew them down the hallway, where a wide archway opened into a room filled with people. The king was sitting on the floor, facing the others. His eyes were closed and he was swaying slowly from side to side, chanting. The rest of the people were copying him. Only the queen, who was seated near the archway, turned to see Annie and Liam. Shaking her head, she held her finger to her lips. Annie and Liam crept away to explore farther down the hall.

They were standing on a balcony that looked over a large interior courtyard when a man with a short beard approached. "I would show you to the room you will be using, should you care to rest," he told them.

The man took them down a different corridor and opened a door, ushering them into a large room with a low table, a few benches against the wall, and a bed on a platform. The bed was covered with brightly colored pillows and was so inviting that Annie was tempted to lie down right then. She made herself wait until the man left, closing the door behind him. Tossing her coat on a bench, she threw herself on the pile of pillows. "This has to be the most comfortable bed ever!" she exclaimed.

"I found something even better," said Liam. "Come look at this!"

Annie groaned and sat up. "It had better be worth it," she told him. "Because this bed is spectacular."

"So is this," Liam said, gesturing to a curtain on the back wall. When he saw that she was watching, he pulled the curtain open, revealing a balcony that looked over the wall surrounding the palace at the mountains beyond. Annie gasped. The view was magnificent.

It hadn't been as easy to see from the ground floor with the wall blocking much of the view, but the palace was built high in the mountains in a valley nestled between three peaks. A pair of eagles soared above the valley. Wispy clouds gathered around the peaks, catching the sunlight in a golden glow that made them look like halos.

"No wonder they find this conducive to meditating," said Annie. "I could look at this all day, too."

"Say, isn't that the meadow that Shareeza told us about?" Liam said, pointing toward a pass not far from the palace. "What would you say about a little walk?"

Annie sighed. She would like nothing better than to relax in the palace, but she knew that Liam preferred action over sitting around. He would get bored quickly, and a bored Liam could be a grumpy Liam. Maybe if they went for a walk now, he would be happy to relax later. "I suppose . . ."

"Good!" said Liam. "We'll have to take our coats. On the way out we can borrow some boots and gloves from that room we found. And I should probably borrow a bow and some arrows. You never know what we might encounter outside the palace walls."

"Do you mean something like a rock dodger?" asked Annie.

"Precisely," Liam said with a grin. "They might be very dangerous."

CHAPTER 5

BOTH ANNIE AND Liam were surprised by how easily they were able to take the items they needed and leave the palace. They found a door with a simple bolt in the wall surrounding the palace and opened it easily. "Where are all the guards?" Liam wondered. They had yet to see a single one.

As Liam closed the door behind them, Annie glanced up. The mountains rose high above, giants in a frozen world. They made Annie feel so small and insignificant that she took Liam's hand for reassurance. The mountains didn't seem to bother him at all. Squeezing her hand, he let it go and took an arrow from the quiver he'd borrowed before starting toward the meadow.

The snow was firmly packed, so they didn't have any problem making their way up the pass. When they finally caught sight of the meadow, Annie cried out in delight. Twists and turns in the mountainside sheltered the meadow from the wind, allowing plants that could stand the cold to flourish. Annie recognized the bobbing white heads of snowdrops, but the rest were all strange to her. She knelt down to examine some pale yellow flowers while Liam searched for rock dodger tracks.

"I found some!" he said after a minute or so. "They're huge! Rock dodgers may be like rabbits, but they're rabbits the size of goats! I'll be right back. These tracks look fresh. I'm going to follow them. I won't go far, so I'll be only a few minutes. Will you be all right?"

"Hmm?" said Annie. "Oh, yes. I'll be fine. I'll be right here when you come back."

The fur coat's hood muffled sounds, so Annie didn't hear Liam leave. She lost all track of time while she examined the flowers, going from one patch to another. Although the air was cold, the heavy fur coat along with the borrowed boots and gloves kept her warm and comfortable. She tried pushing the hood back because it limited her vision, but her ears became painfully cold right away. *Better to have tunnel vision than to have my ears freeze,* she thought, and pulled the hood up again.

Annie was bending over a tiny blue flower when she heard a high-pitched yowl behind her. She turned quickly just as two enormous, furry white arms snatched her off the ground. Annie squirmed, shouting, as whatever held her straightened up and started walking. She beat at the arms and tried to pry them off her, but the only response was a gentle squeeze and a muffled grunt.

When her captor turned enough that Annie could look behind her, she saw a group of tall, white-furred beings who looked like oversize, fuzzy humans crossing through the meadow. One that was well over eight feet tall had a snow leopard in its arms and was squeezing it into submission. Spitting and snarling, the leopard fought the embrace. Suddenly it went limp and the creature dropped it on the ground, where it lay still. Annie stopped struggling then, afraid she'd receive the same treatment. Thinking that the creature holding her might put her down if she went limp, she relaxed and closed her eyes like the leopard. Instead of putting her down, however, the creature changed its grip so that it was cradling Annie like a baby and started walking.

After a few minutes, Annie opened her eyes just enough that she could see her captor's face. Its features were coarse and covered with fur, but it had kind eyes when it glanced down and saw Annie looking up at it. The creature began to hum and rock Annie in its arms. Although she was terrified and worried about what might have happened to Liam, Annie felt herself growing drowsy. Before she knew it, she had drifted off to sleep.

꙳

When Annie woke, she was lying on a bed of soft, dried grass. One of the creatures was seated beside her with its back to her. Annie had no way of knowing if it was the same creature that had carried her or not. More frightened that she'd ever been in her life, Annie didn't move. It wasn't long, however, before her curiosity grew too strong to ignore. Without sitting up or letting on that she was awake, Annie looked around. She discovered that they were in a cave filled with furry, white creatures, all of whom seemed to be waiting for something. When she glanced at the cave opening, she saw that it was snowing, but still daylight. *Perhaps they're waiting for the snow to stop*, thought Annie.

It occurred to her that Liam might have been captured, too, but she didn't hear him and couldn't see much as long as she was lying down. She grew more anxious as time passed and finally couldn't stand it any longer. As soon as she sat up, the creature beside her turned her way and smiled. Making soft sounds in its throat, the creature handed her a hollowed-out gourd filled with water. Annie was too thirsty to turn it down. She took a big sip, then another, trying not to think about who or what had used the gourd before her. When she was finished, she handed the gourd back to the creature, who patted Annie's head and smiled again.

Now the other creatures were aware that Annie was awake. They came by one at a time to look at her and make quizzical grunts at their friend sitting beside her. Some of them made sounds that sounded like "Mara," so Annie began to consider that her captor's name. She wondered if Mara was a female; her movements were more graceful than some of the bigger adults and her gestures more refined.

While Mara was occupied, Annie looked around for Liam. As far as she could tell, he wasn't there.

Annie turned back when a different creature brought a bit of brown fur and handed it to Mara. After examining it, she gave it to Annie, smiling. It was a crude doll made of scraps of fur. Another creature brought something small and white. Mara examined it as well before handing Annie a ring made of bone. Although other creatures brought other gifts, Mara rejected most of them; the only other one she passed on to Annie was a pretty blue stone shot with gold.

Annie accepted all the gifts, examining them out of curiosity. She was looking at the stone when another creature gave something to Mara. Annie's captor sniffed it and handed it to Annie. It was raw meat, still warm and steaming in the cold air.

Shaking her head, she handed it back to Mara, who looked worried and tried to give it to her again. Annie refused to take it. She shrank back when other creatures came to stare at her and make soft grunts at Mara. Although they didn't seem to mean any harm, it worried Annie. If so many were watching her, how would she ever get away?

When Mara called out, a smaller creature came to see her, looking at her with bright, expectant eyes. It was eager to accept the piece of meat that Annie had turned down, and it gave Annie a quizzical look as it chewed. Annie noticed that the small one was about her own size and was covered with cream-colored fur, the same color as Annie's coat. Its face was nearly as bare as Annie's, with only a slight dusting of fur on the cheeks, forehead, and chin. Although its nose was flatter, its eyes were set farther apart, and its lips were very narrow, without the fur it might have passed for human. Annie couldn't be sure, but she had a feeling that the little creature was a girl.

When Annie looked around, she saw other smaller creatures. A thought occurred to her, and suddenly she knew it was true. *The smaller ones with cream-colored fur are children. The creatures think that I'm a child as well!*

But why would they carry off a strange child like this? she wondered. *Perhaps they thought they were rescuing one that was abandoned or orphaned.* Watching the adults with the children, she saw how much the creatures treasured the little ones. Mara didn't consider herself Annie's captor; she was her protector! She'd been making sure her friends were giving Annie only the choicest of toys and best piece of meat.

Annie wondered if she could use this to her advantage. Holding up the fur doll, she showed it to the little girl. The little girl smiled and ran off, grabbed something from where she'd been sitting before, and brought it back to show Annie. It was a doll, just like the one Annie was holding. Mara looked on indulgently when the little girl plopped down beside Annie and made soft sounds while wiggling the doll, as if her doll were talking to Annie's. They played like that for a few minutes, then the child jumped up and pulled Annie to her feet. They chased each other around the cave while Mara watched anxiously from the side. When Annie was in the lead, she ran toward the cave entrance, turning back just before she reached it when she heard Mara call out. She did this again and again, until finally Mara wasn't looking and she was able to run out the opening while the only one watching was the little girl.

Annie ran through the still-falling snow, not having any idea where she was or where she was going. The snow was getting deeper, however, and her feet sank in a few inches with every step. When she left the shelter of the rocks that surrounded the cave, she found that the snow was so thick that she had to slog through it.

Running was no longer possible. She had stopped, trying to decide what to do next, when Mara picked her up once again and hugged her. Escaping wasn't going to be easy with a watchful protector and no idea where to go even if she could get away.

Once again, Mara carried her to the cave and sat down beside her. Annie was frustrated and close to tears. She couldn't stay here any longer, not knowing where Liam was or if he was all right. But how could she get away? Mara wasn't going to let her go as long as she thought Annie was a little one who needed her protection. Somehow, Annie was going to have to let them know that she wasn't a child of their species. But how? They didn't talk the way she did, so she couldn't really tell them. Maybe she could show them instead.

Annie tapped Mara on the shoulder to get her attention. When Mara was looking directly at her, Annie reached up and pulled off her hood. The reaction she got wasn't at all what she'd expected.

Mara screamed! It was a horrible, horrifying scream like one would make if a monster appeared in the dead of night. *Or,* thought Annie, *like a person who had just seen a loved one pull off the top of her head.* Suddenly, the other creatures were screaming and Annie had to cover her ears because it was so loud. When a deeper voice roared, they all stopped and the silence was almost as awful.

Annie was already wishing she'd thought of another way to tell Mara when one of the largest creatures came to where she was sitting. The creature glared at her, poked at her hood with its furry hand, and grunted at Mara. Making noises deep in their throats, they had a conversation that Annie couldn't follow. When they stopped and the bigger creature stalked away, Mara got to her feet with tears welling from her eyes.

Annie didn't move as Mara gently pulled the hood over her hair. She looked so sad that Annie felt awful. The creatures in the cave watched as Mara picked up Annie and carried her from the cave, but not one of them offered to go with her. The wind was fierce when they got out into the open, and Annie was forced to bury her face in Mara's fur as they made their way down the mountain.

Annie lost track of time as they struggled through the storm. When Mara finally set her down, Annie found herself back in the meadow where she had been looking at the flowers. It was dusk, and although she had half hoped that Liam would be there waiting for her, she hadn't really expected it. No one was there, however, and she couldn't help but feel disappointed.

Annie looked up when she felt Mara pat her on the back. The creature was already walking away when Annie ran after her and threw her arms around her.

Mara wasn't human, but she had shown Annie more affection in one day than her mother had for most of Annie's life. When the creature returned the hug, neither one was in a hurry to let go.

The wind was dying down and the snow had finally stopped falling when Mara stepped back. Before she left, she handed Annie the doll, the bone ring, and the stone. Annie wanted to give her something in return, so she took off a bracelet that she'd had for years and handed it to her new friend. They stood for a moment, looking into each other's eyes, before Mara turned and walked away.

Annie's eyes were as red as Mara's when she started down the slope toward the castle.

ॐ

Liam met her when she was halfway down the slope. "Annie!" he called when he saw her. They hurried toward each other as fast as they could in the deep snow. "I've been looking everywhere for you! Where did you go?"

Before Annie could answer, he was there, hugging her until her ribs ached and kissing her so hard that her lips felt bruised.

"I never should have left you alone!" Liam said. "Something awful could have happened to you! I came back when it started to snow, and you were gone. I was hoping you'd found a cave for shelter. These mountains are riddled with them. I found one myself and stayed there for the whole storm."

"I was in a cave," said Annie. "But it wasn't anywhere near here." She told him all about being abducted and finding out that her captors thought they were rescuing her. Liam was angry then—at himself for leaving her, and at the creatures for taking her. When she described the creatures, he admitted that he'd never heard of such beings before.

"I'm sure the king can tell us about them," Liam told her. "Let's go back to our room. You need a hot bath and some rest."

A bath sounded good to Annie. She knew that she smelled musky and slightly acrid like Mara, and was glad that Liam was gentleman enough not to mention it.

༄

Annie sank lower in the tub and groaned. The hot water felt wonderful, and she loved the perfume and rose petals the servants had poured into the water. She had been surprised when the serving woman had led her to this room just down the hall and shown her the tub big enough for a small family. *This kingdom is full of surprises*, thought Annie.

She stayed in the tub until her muscles had relaxed and the water was getting cold. When she climbed out, she dried herself off and put on the loose gown that the woman had left for her. The woman had left a jeweled band for her hair, as well, which Annie used to hold it back. Gathering up her dirty clothes, she returned to the room that she and Liam were sharing and lay down on the pillow-covered bed. She fell asleep instantly and was still sleeping when there was a knock on the door and Liam answered it.

"His Majesty King Lalidama requests your presence in the dining hall. I am to accompany you."

Annie woke up enough to recognize the voice of the bearded man who had shown them to their room. She sat up, the thought of food making her aware of how hungry she was and how little she'd eaten that day. While Liam opened the door just enough to talk to the man, she crawled off the bed and changed into her own clothes. The people who lived in Westerling might wear loose gowns, but Annie didn't really feel dressed unless she was wearing her own undergarments and a fitted gown with lacing.

Annie was brushing her hair when Liam asked the man to wait and closed the door. "I thought you were asleep!" he said when he saw her.

"I was, but the man's voice woke me. I'll be ready in just a minute," Annie told him.

"Here, let me help with that," Liam said, taking the brush from her hand. He brushed her hair, gently working out the snarls while she stood with her head tilted back. "I went to see the king to tell him what had happened, but he was still meditating. We'll talk to him at supper."

Annie tried to hold her head still as the brush tugged at her hair. "It seems almost like a dream now."

"Don't move," said Liam. "I'm almost done."

When he was finished, Annie caught up her hair in the band again and turned to smile at him. "I wish you would do that every day," she said, and gave him a kiss.

Tossing the brush on the bed, Liam pulled Annie into his arms and returned her kiss with one that was long and slow. They didn't move apart until there was another knock on the door. When Liam raised his head, Annie's breath was ragged and her cheeks were flushed.

"I'd be happy to do this every day," Liam said with a smile.

They went to the door together and followed the obviously impatient man down the stairs to the dining hall. It was a bigger room than the one they had eaten in before and was already filled with people standing around the long, low tables. The bearded man positioned them at the head table before leaving the room. Annie could feel the eyes of everyone in the hall on her. Although it made her fidget, it didn't seem to bother Liam.

Less than a minute later, everyone stood at a signal from the man with the beard. King Lalidama strode in through another doorway with Queen Shareeza on his arm. Going to the head table, they smiled graciously at the people in the room. As soon as the king and queen took their seats, everyone else sat as well. The room rustled with the sound of fabric on fabric as people made themselves comfortable on the floor pillows, but no one spoke until the king lifted his glass of crystal clear water, took a sip, and nodded. Then everyone began to talk in a low murmur.

There were only two other people at the head table besides the royal couple, and Annie and Liam. One was a middle-aged man with a military bearing; the other was his wife, who looked down her nose at the servants and barely spared Annie a second glance. Liam smiled and spoke to them as easily as if he had known them for years, and they were both soon talking and laughing with him. Even so, Annie could tell that Liam was waiting for his chance to talk to the king, who was holding a quiet conversation with his wife.

Annie was nibbling a piece of pickled fruit, listening to Liam's conversation, when Queen Shareeza turned to her and said, "I'm curious. What did you do all day?"

"We explored, as you suggested," said Annie. "Your palace is even lovelier than I realized. I could see how it would be conducive to meditating," she added, glancing at the king. "And then we went to the meadow you mentioned. It's extraordinary that so many flowers can bloom in the snow."

"You did what?" the queen said, turning a shade paler. The king glanced at Annie, the first time he'd done so since sitting down to eat.

"I saw a lot of tracks for the rock dodgers you told us about," Liam said, entering the conversation. "But I didn't see a single animal."

"You went outside the palace walls?" said the king, an odd note to his voice.

"We did," said Annie. "And the most extraordinary thing happened. Liam was just out of sight when some creatures came along. One of them picked me up and carried me off. They took me to a cave where we waited out the storm. They were actually quite nice to me. One brought me back to the meadow after the storm was over."

Annie had the strangest feeling as soon as she started telling her story. Something wasn't right, but she couldn't imagine what. From the horrified looks on their faces, she thought they might be worried about her safety, but they only seemed to get more upset as her story progressed.

"Annie and I have never heard about creatures like these," said Liam. "They were big, you said, and covered with white fur, right, Annie?"

"Yes, and the males were bigger than the females. The children were—"

"Enough!" roared the king. "You come uninvited to our home on one of our holiest of days and violate the taboo that no one has challenged in a thousand years. No one can be as ignorant as you claim to be. Everyone knows what a yeti looks like! And everyone knows that you do not go outside the palace walls during Shumra, the heart of the yeti migration. To do so means certain death. It also means that you scorn our laws and traditions. Wasn't it enough that you didn't join us in meditation? But to make up lies and call the yetis kindly beasts is inconceivable! Yetis are terrible monsters that spring from the snow itself. They are solitary monsters; there are no yeti females or children. There is only one kind of yeti, and they do not protect girls in snowstorms. You mock our beliefs on our holiest of days! Go! Leave my table. You are no longer welcome guests in my home. Guards! Take them back to the room they are using and make sure they do not leave. And take that medallion from Prince Liam. They cannot use magic to escape what they have done. Deeds like this do not go unpunished. I will meditate and decide your fate tonight."

Annie was aghast. She and Liam hadn't been lying, nor had they meant to be disrespectful. No one had told them that they shouldn't go outside the palace walls. Nor had they ever heard about yetis before. She got to her feet even as a man in a loose gray robe jerked the medallion off Liam's neck and turned him toward the door. When another gray-robed man reached for Annie, she hurried after Liam, not wanting the guards to touch her.

Liam took Annie's hand as the guards hustled them up the stairs. They were moving so fast that she would have tripped if he hadn't held her upright. When they reached the room, the guards shoved them inside and closed the door. The scrape of the lock seemed loud in the silence that followed.

"So there were guards after all," Liam said as he reached into his pocket.

"And they must use the weapons we found in that room on the yetis," said Annie. "Poor creatures. They aren't nearly what the king claimed them to be. No females or children? How can these people live in their midst and know so little about them?"

"Fear, most likely," said Liam. "But we're not going to stick around to talk to them. It's time we moved on. Ready?"

"Let me get our coats," said Annie. She ran to the bench where they'd left them and was back a few seconds later. "Now we can go."

Liam held out the next postcard. Together, they touched the center and vanished.

CHAPTER 6

IT MIGHT HAVE been hard to tell where they were when they arrived at their next destination if the sky hadn't been clear. Although it was night, the multitude of stars twinkling overhead allowed Annie and Liam to see for miles.

"Look at that!" said Annie. "It's amazing!"

"We're in the desert," said Liam. "There's nothing to block our view except the city over there. It must be the one in the postcard, but it looks very different at night."

Annie looked where he was pointing and nodded. "You can't see much of it now, can you? The castle is well lit, but the city isn't." She shivered and handed Liam his coat. "We should put these on. It's cold here. I would have thought a desert would be hotter than this."

"Not at night," Liam said as he pulled on his coat. "I wish I knew what kingdom this is. It must be far from

Treecrest and Dorinocco. The stars aren't in the same places as they are at home."

"Let's go find out," said Annie. "There's a road over this way."

"I hope they'll open the gate for us this late at night," Liam told her.

They had to be careful where they placed their feet on the uneven ground at first, but once they reached the road, they were able to look around while they walked. There was a wall around the city, which didn't look very big but grew larger and larger as they drew closer. A castle prickly with spires loomed over the tallest buildings like a monster hovering over its prey. Some of the spires were ablaze with lights, while others were so dark, they were visible only because they blocked the stars behind them. Annie thought the castle was the ugliest building she'd ever seen, and wondered why the woods witch had included it in the postcards.

They had almost reached the wall when a *whoomp! whoomp!* overhead made Annie look up. Something long and narrow was flying toward the castle on enormous wings; Annie had never seen anything like it. "What is that?" she asked Liam.

"I can't tell from here," said Liam. "There's no one at the gate, but there's a door in the wall. Let's try that. Maybe someone will come if we knock."

Raising his fist, he banged on the door, shouting, "Let us in!" When no one came right away, Annie raised her voice with his and started pounding. After a few minutes, a small slot squeaked open in the door, revealing a tiny peephole. A moment later, an eye filled the hole.

"What do you want?" demanded a man's deep voice.

"We want to come in," said Liam.

"Go away. We're not letting anyone in tonight."

The peephole closed partway, then seemed to get stuck. Fingers fumbled with the cover as someone tried to close it the rest of the way. Annie could hear the man who had been rude talking to someone else, although she could hear only his side of the conversation.

"No, I didn't ask anything about them. What difference would it make? I'm not letting them in no matter what pitiful story they tell me. Yes, I heard the captain's orders. I know he said to keep an eye open. What? You think it might be them? Let me take another look."

The cover to the peephole squeaked again and the eye reappeared. "Why are you here?" the man barked when he saw Annie.

She glanced at Liam, then back at the eye. "We just got married and we're on our grand tour and—"

The eye disappeared. There was a muffled conversation on the other side of the door before the voice said, "All right! You may enter." The man forced the peephole cover closed, and there was a loud scraping sound. He grunted and cursed under his breath as he dragged the heavy door open. Annie could see why the task was so difficult when they stepped through the opening. The man was no more than four feet tall and looked as if he'd have to hold on to something heavy whenever a strong wind blew. His companion was the same size and had the same swarthy skin and bumpy nose. Annie suspected that they were twins.

Liam helped them close the door, which revealed a large box that the guard had used to stand on. When the door was closed and barricaded, the guard who had been talking to them said, "You have to stay here until the captain comes. He wants to see you."

"Why?" Liam asked.

The guard shrugged. "How should I know? He doesn't confide in me! Timmon, you go tell him that they're here while I keep an eye on them."

His twin nodded and ran off, leaving the first guard staring at Annie and Liam. "Now, don't you get any ideas about overpowering me. I may be short, but I'm fast!" he said, emphasizing his words with a few quick jabs at the air.

"We wouldn't dream of it," Liam said without a trace of a smile.

A bell pealed somewhere in the city. At the first note, the guard's expression changed from belligerent to frightened.

"What is it?" asked Annie.

"Dragons!" people screamed as a building a few blocks away erupted in flames. A series of explosions made the ground shake. Annie held her breath when an enormous lizard-like beast flew overhead, blocking the stars for a moment. Its scales glowed red in the reflected firelight. Another, paler dragon flew beside it. Opening its mouth, it exhaled a cloud that ignited when the first dragon blew fire at it. Together they blew up buildings on the next street over.

"It looks as if there are two kinds of dragons," Liam told Annie. "The one that puffs some kind of gas and the one that breathes fire that ignites the gas. They make a nasty combination."

The guard who was supposed to be watching Annie and Liam was growing more and more agitated. People carrying water-filled buckets ran by, hurrying to put out the fires. "Jimmie, come help!" shouted one.

"I can't," the guard yelled back. "I have to stay here."

"We need you!"

"I can't . . . I just . . . ," Jimmie said, the two choices warring inside him. When a woman screamed, Jimmie turned to Annie and Liam, saying, "Listen, I have to go. You two stay here until I get back."

The guard ran off, disappearing down the street, where a new fire was raging. A moment later, a slender white dragon swooped low over Annie and Liam, blowing mist at a building close to where they stood. Another, bigger dragon followed the first, breathing a long tongue of flame into the mist. The air above the building exploded, knocking off the roof and setting the rest on fire.

"We're not staying here!" Liam shouted, sheltering Annie as debris hailed down around them. "We have to get to the castle and see if we can help the king."

Annie and Liam ran toward the center of the city, dodging flaming pieces of roofing, volunteers hauling buckets, and terrified families running in the opposite direction. When they ran into soldiers shooting arrows at the dragons, they turned down another street. Soon they were seeing soldiers everywhere, running through the streets or trying to shoot down dragons.

Annie and Liam were running past a small shop on a road leading to the castle gate when three men ran out of the building. Annie tried to go around a man in the middle of the road, but he ran straight at her, grabbed her around her waist, and dragged her into the building.

"Liam!" she screamed as the other two men jumped him.

Annie didn't see what happened to Liam after that, because the man holding her forced her into the shop. There were other men inside, but none of them came to help her.

"Quiet!" the stranger told her when she continued to cry out. "Your young man will be here soon enough. You don't want to attract the people looking for you, do you? Like the soldiers who plan to march you off to a dungeon cell?"

It took a moment for the man's words to sink in. When they did, Annie stopped trying to get away and said, "Someone is looking for us? How is that possible? We didn't even know we were coming here until we arrived."

"Let me explain," a man said from the shadows in the back of the shop. He walked into the light from one of the two lanterns as he talked. Even before she could see him, Annie guessed he was the leader from the way the others looked at him and moved aside to let him pass. "I work in the castle and I overheard King Beltran with a visitor who claimed to be a wizard. The man said he wanted to warn the king that two spies pretending to be on their grand tour were about to arrive."

Everyone turned as Liam burst into the room, armed with a sword he'd taken from one of his attackers. When he saw the men surrounding Annie, he pointed the sword at the man closest to her and said, "Stay still, Annie, my love. This will take just a minute."

"No, Liam! Wait! They have something to tell us. Please go on," she told the leader.

"You and your young man fit the description that the wizard gave perfectly. The king has had his guards looking for you ever since the wizard was here. Apparently the only thing the wizard didn't tell him was when you would arrive. Beltran plans to throw you in his dungeon and torture you until you tell him who sent you, then have you both executed. He believes that you have been sent to assassinate him."

"That's ridiculous!" said Annie. "We really are on our grand tour!"

Liam had made his way to Annie's side. Turning to the leader, he said, "Did you hear this wizard's name? Can you tell us what he looks like?"

"I didn't hear his name, but I can tell you that he's balder than a baby's bottom. He's got bushy eyebrows and long nose hairs. Oh, and his eyes are small and close together."

"Rotan!" Annie and Liam said at the same time.

Annie glanced at Liam. "How does he know where we're going?"

Liam shrugged. "He must have talked to the woods witch. So much for Moonbeam taking care of him for us."

"So you really aren't assassins or spies?" asked the leader.

Annie shook her head. "We just got married. We're taking a trip before we settle down."

"That's too bad," said a man with a straggly beard. "We would have been happy to help you assassinate Beltran. Are you sure you wouldn't like to give it a try?"

"You hate your king that much?" asked Liam.

"King? Pah! He took over when his brother died of mysterious causes. Beltran has involved East Aridia in one war after another ever since."

73

"My brother was turned into a mouse when Beltran made the army fight in Greater Greensward," declared the man who had grabbed Annie. "He's back now, but he still has an unquenchable desire to eat cheese."

"And now Beltran has gotten us into a war with dragons!" said the bearded man. "Not just one kind, either. The fire-breathing dragons and the ice dragons used to hate each other, but now they're allied against us because Beltran is so greedy."

"He tried to take over the mine where the dragons dig up their gems. Dragons don't take kindly to being robbed," the leader told them.

"He doesn't sound like the kind of person who would listen if we tried to explain why we're here," Annie said to Liam.

"If you value your life, you won't go anywhere near him," said the leader. "The man is insane."

"Unless they want to help us assassinate him, in which case we could get them in the room with him," said the bearded man. "And supply them with weapons."

"We're not here to assassinate anyone," said Liam. "Or to get mixed up in your kingdom's affairs!"

"We never should have come here," Annie told him.

Liam nodded. "I know. And there's no good reason to stay. If you gentlemen will excuse us," he said, and took Annie's hand.

"Not so fast," said the bearded man. "I think we can use them. What if one of us dressed as a guard and took them in? Beltran wants to see them, so our man could take these two all the way to his private rooms. When he's in Beltran's presence, he could kill the king and whoever is with him."

"And leave us to take the blame?" said Liam. "I don't think so!"

"Maybe it isn't your decision to make," said the man who had grabbed Annie. He took a step toward her, looking anything but friendly.

"I think we should help if we can," Annie hurried to say. "Let me talk to my husband. If you gentlemen will give us just a moment?"

The men exchanged glances, then the leader nodded and the others backed off. Annie led Liam to the side of the room, ignoring the angry look on his face. She turned so that her back was to the wall and he was facing her.

"Postcard," she whispered.

Understanding erased the anger from his face. Annie didn't want to help these men any more than he did. She was giving them a moment together, and a moment was all they needed. While the men began to grow impatient, Liam reached into his pocket for a postcard. They both touched it and were gone.

CHAPTER 7

THEY WERE IN a desert again. As far as Annie could tell, it might even be the same one. The stars still twinkled overhead, a cool breeze was making her pull her coat closer around her, and sand was once again filling her shoes. "Are we still in East Aridia?" she asked Liam.

"We're nowhere near East Aridia," he said, looking at the sky. "See those stars? I recognize some of the constellations, although they aren't in the same places as they would be at home. When we were in East Aridia, none of the constellations were familiar."

Annie shivered. "Wherever we are, it's as cold here as it was there. Do you see anywhere we can get out of this wind? I'm cold and tired and would like to get some sleep."

Liam lowered his eyes to the land around them. "I think I see trees over there," he said, pointing.

"In the desert?" said Annie. "I see shapes, but I can't tell what they are."

Although there was a full moon, it wasn't enough to see the shapes clearly, so they started walking to investigate. "How odd," Liam said when they drew closer. "They might be trees, but they're not like any I've ever seen." The unusual plants grew to well over their heads, with trunks covered with overlapping scales and fern-like growths at the top.

"Look, there are a lot more in this direction," said Annie. "And I think I see the moon reflecting off water."

They found a small lake at the edge of the plants. When Liam scooped up some water to taste, he declared it fresh and pure. They drank then, wishing they had something to eat. Annie was now so tired that she couldn't stop yawning, so Liam took his coat and spread it on the ground at the base of one of the odd plants. After Annie lay down on the fur coat, Liam sat down beside her and used Annie's coat to cover them. The coats smelled of dragon fire and burning buildings, and weren't long enough to cover Annie's feet, but she was thankful that they had them.

"Aren't you going to lie down?" she asked Liam.

"I'd sleep too soundly if I did. I can doze if I'm sitting up, but I'll still hear if anyone or anything comes close." He patted the sword he'd placed across his lap. Annie recognized it as the sword he'd taken from one of the men who'd jumped him in East Aridia. At least now they weren't completely defenseless.

"Have you noticed that every place we've visited through the postcards has turned out to be dangerous one way or another?" said Annie.

"I've noticed," Liam replied. "The trolls attacked at Delaroo Pass, then the yetis kidnapped you in Westerling, although I think that the people at Westerling were more dangerous than the beasts."

"I think so, too," Annie said, and yawned.

"The dragons and the rebellion in East Aridia made that the worst place to visit."

Annie shuddered. "I don't ever want to go back there again. But do you think Holly, the woods witch, gave us cards for dangerous places on purpose, or is every interesting place dangerous?"

"Good question," said Liam. "Then again, Delaroo Pass wasn't really dangerous until after your presence made the magic of the wall stop working."

"I might have thought that was an accident if my effect on magic weren't common knowledge now. Holly could have known about the layout at Delaroo Pass and what I do to magic, which means she did it on purpose. But if Holly rarely talked to people, like she said, it's possible that she didn't know about me."

"Maybe," said Liam. "There's another possibility and it might explain how Rotan knew where we were headed. Do you think he could have disguised himself as Holly and given us those cards?"

"That's a scary thought! But I don't think so. I think he would have given himself away with the details. I was watching her because I thought she was delightfully odd, and I would have noticed if something didn't make sense. Holly was too real to be a man in disguise."

"Unless Rotan was the best actor in all the kingdoms, which I doubt very much. I don't think he's smart enough!" said Liam. "I have to say, however, that a lot of things have been odd ever since Holly showed up. You seeing your uncle for the first time. The yetis showing their true selves to you when the people who live near them don't know the real yetis at all. And what about East Aridia? It must be really far from Treecrest if there are dragons there."

"One of the men in East Aridia mentioned Greater Greensward," said Annie. "I've never heard of that kingdom, either. And remember how he said his brother was turned into a mouse? It sounds like a dreadful place. That poor man! I know I would hate it! I hope we don't go there, but if we don't know what the places on the postcards are called, it's hard to avoid the ones we don't want to see. Some of the kingdoms the postcards take us to aren't at all nice."

"I wish I knew where we are now," said Liam.

"Have you looked at all the postcards?" asked Annie. "Is there one that could take us home?"

Liam shook his head. "No, there isn't, at least not that I can tell. I'm sorry, Annie. I should have looked at them more closely before we started this whole thing. I'm sorry I got us into this mess!"

"It's not a mess, Liam," Annie said. "It's an adventure! We'll look at the cards together in the morning. I'm sure we'll find our way home somehow."

≈

"Annie," Liam whispered just loud enough for her to hear. "We have company."

Annie opened her eyes. The sun was up, although it had yet to rise very high in the sky. A brightly colored bird with a long, streaming tail flew over them. Annie glanced at Liam, but he wasn't looking at her or the bird. He was looking past her and he didn't seem happy.

Annie turned her head and saw a pair of feet wearing simple leather shoes peeking out from under a dusty robe. She looked again and realized that there were two pairs of feet, and they were attached to two men with scowling faces and long, curved swords. She sat up abruptly and inched closer to Liam.

One of the men said something in a language Annie didn't understand and pointed at Liam's sword with his own. "I think he wants you to put your sword aside," Annie whispered.

"I got that," said Liam. Moving slowly, he set the sword on the ground and stood up. Annie reached for his hand and he pulled her up beside him.

While one of the men held his sword in a threatening way, the other picked up Liam's sword and the two coats. When he gestured for Annie and Liam to start walking, they turned and set out along the edge of the lake.

"Should we use the postcard now?" whispered Annie.

"Not until we're alone," Liam said under his breath. "I have a feeling they could cut us in two with those swords before I got my hand out of my pocket."

Liam stumbled and Annie looked behind them. One of the men was prodding him between the shoulder blades with his curved sword. Annie closed her mouth, certain that Liam was right.

The shore line angled back, revealing that the lake was much bigger than Annie had first thought. She almost said something to Liam, but after a quick glance behind her, she held her tongue again. The man was still holding his sword inches from Liam's back and she didn't want to give him any excuse to use it.

They followed the curve of the lake, and it wasn't long before she spotted a large group of tents set up at the water's edge. The biggest, most elaborate tent faced a shallow beach, while smaller tents surrounded it on the other three sides. Skirting the first of the tents, the men made Annie and Liam walk to a smaller one set well away from the water. After lifting the tent flap and looking inside, they gestured for Annie and Liam to enter.

As soon as they were inside, one of the men pantomimed emptying out their pockets. Annie didn't like handing over the gifts from the yetis, but she was far more upset that Liam had to give them the postcards. After a cursory glance at the cards, the men became excited when they saw the blue stone that Mara's friend had given to Annie and talked to each other in excited voices. Although Annie still couldn't understand them, she did hear one word that she recognized and it made her heart sink. Shooting odd looks at Annie, the men left the tent and closed the flap behind them.

Annie and Liam were in the near dark with just a small amount of light filtering through gaps in the tent seams. The quick glimpse Annie had gotten before the men left had shown her that it was empty, without a single piece of furniture or rug or cushion to sit on. "Now what?" she said, turning to Liam. "Without the postcards, we have no way to leave, and possibly no way to get home."

"It's not all bad," Liam said, taking her hand in his. "They didn't cut off our heads yet, which probably means they're waiting for someone in authority. We just need to talk to someone who speaks the same language, and we can explain our situation."

"I have a feeling that I know who that someone might be, and it isn't good. When they were talking, one of them mentioned Nasheen. Unless that's a common name around here, we might just be in Viramoot about to face its crown prince. The last time we saw Nasheen in Snow White's castle, he was furious. I don't think we'll get a very friendly reception if it is him."

"Nasheen, huh?" said Liam. "He was a bad sport and not very friendly, and that was when he was trying to make a good impression. I can only imagine what he'd be like now. They don't seem to take too kindly to visitors here. Nasheen may not want to cut off our heads, but I don't think we should stick around to find out. Maybe we should see if there's a way out of this tent. It wouldn't be easy without a weapon or any supplies, but we could head east and make our way to Helmswood. I'm sure Snow White and her father would help us get home from there."

Annie nodded, even though Liam couldn't see her. "The ground is sand, so we should be able to dig a hole under the tent big enough that we can squeeze through."

"That's what I was thinking," said Liam. "We'll start here, across from the opening."

Although the ground was sand, it was compacted and as hard as rock. They were scraping at it as best they could without any tools when they heard the commotion of returning riders. Voices called out, horses whinnied, and hooves thundered past as the group of riders rode to the center of the encampment.

"Do you think that's Nasheen?" Annie asked.

"Probably, the way our luck has been running," said Liam. "I wish I had my knife with me. It would have ruined the blade, but I could have used it to dig a hole by now."

Although it seemed fruitless, Annie and Liam kept scraping at the ground, hoping that they might actually make a hole if they were given enough time. The tent was stuffy and unbearably hot when the two men threw open the flap and gestured for them to come out.

Annie was sweaty and had a pounding headache when she stepped into the sunlight. She shaded her eyes against the bright light, while Liam did the same. The sun beat down on them as the men took them between the tents, although the air grew cooler when they drew closer to the lake. They entered the big tent through an opening at the end and knew right away that the occupant was royalty. Everything inside was luxurious, from the thick, patterned rugs to the wall hangings depicting stylized hunting scenes. Passing between two curtains, they entered a larger

84

room filled with low tables, gilded stools, and cushion-covered benches that were only inches above the floor. Lanterns made of pierced gold hung from the ceiling, along with golden cages where colorful birds hopped from perch to perch.

Two guards stood by the large opening in the tent wall facing the lake. Eyeing Annie and Liam with suspicion, they turned to lead the way out of the tent to a table set up at the water's edge. Three other guards stood near the table, where a man in shimmering robes was sitting by himself. As they approached, Annie got a good look at the man's profile. It was Prince Nasheen, a man she'd hoped she'd never see again.

The prince didn't look up right away. While they waited in silence, Annie braced herself for his anger or at least his dislike. When he finally looked up, she was surprised that he actually seemed pleased to see them.

"Princess Annabelle! Prince Liam! What are you doing here?" asked Nasheen. "My men said they found two vagabonds asleep beside my lake."

"We're on our grand tour, actually," said Annie. "We got married a few days ago."

"Good for you! I knew you would sooner or later. Has Snow White married that prince whose name I never can remember?"

"Prince Maitland?" said Annie. "No, they're still planning their wedding."

Prince Nasheen sighed. "I wish them well. It seems everyone is getting married but me. I hope to remedy that soon, however. I'm glad you're here. Perhaps you can help me the way you helped Snow White, Annabelle. I know you were behind her contest."

"You want to hold a contest?" asked Liam.

"No, no! Nothing like that! I already know whom I want to marry. Ah! Where are my manners? Please be seated and help yourself to my humble breakfast. There should be enough for three." Platters of fresh fruit and bowls of nuts vied for space with pungent sausages, boiled eggs floating in butter, and tiny fish cooked in oil. The prince gestured to servants hidden out of sight behind curtains. They came running, bringing benches, plates, and cups for Annie and Liam.

With a nod and a wave of his hand, Nasheen dismissed the servants and the guards. "You have arrived at a most favorable time," he told Annie and Liam. "I have fallen in love and wish to marry my angel as soon as it can be arranged. There is only one problem. It is a small detail, really, and something that I'm sure you can help me handle. Sarina, the love of my life, acts as if she doesn't know that I exist. She has many suitors, but only one is a handsome prince."

"You?" said Annie.

"Yes, of course I speak of myself!" the prince said, looking indignant.

"And how can I help you with that?" asked Annie.

86

"That is for you to tell me!" replied Nasheen. "Sarina is the only daughter of a fabulously wealthy merchant. Her father dotes on her and sees that she wants for nothing. She is beautiful, charming, smart, funny, kind, generous, unselfish . . . all the things I want in my future wife. And because her father came into his wealth only recently, she has all of these attributes naturally, not because fairies gave them to her. Rather like you, Annabelle, only much prettier, sweeter, and oh, so much better!"

"Gee, thanks!" said Annie.

"You helped the princess Snow White find her one true love," said Nasheen. "Can you help Sarina see that I am hers? If you do, I will give you anything your heart desires! If you fail me, however, I might be so busy trying to woo her on my own that I could forget you are here and not notice that my men have shut you in that little tent, hot and thirsty, for a very long time."

"I'd be happy to do whatever I can to help you, Nasheen! Tell me, what else do you know about her?"

"I have told you everything you need to know!" said Nasheen.

"Not if I'm going to help you," Annie replied. "You need to find out what she likes and dislikes. Is there anything she dreams of doing someday? What attributes does she value in a person?"

"Does all that really matter?" asked Nasheen.

87

Annie nodded. "Very much. You find out the answers and I can help you."

"That is nothing," Nasheen said, waving his hand as if shooing away a fly. "I can have my servants learn the answers to those questions. Now tell me what *I* must do."

Annie had never considered herself an expert on love, but she had learned a few things when helping others. While trying to wake her sister from a curse, Annie had taken part in a contest that Prince Andreas had held to find a bride. She had won the contest because she saw how important shared interests were to the prince. "You need to know what she likes and show her that you are interested in the same kinds of things," Annie began. Her friend Snow White had wanted to marry a young man who loved her for herself. "Show her that you really know and care about her." Glancing at Liam, she added what had made her fall in love with her own prince. "Be good to her and let her know how special you think she is. Be honest and true and brave at all times."

"Those are all easy things to do!" Nasheen announced. "I am already all of the good things you mentioned. This is much easier than what I had planned."

"What was that?" asked Liam.

"Perhaps you have not noticed that I have had my tent placed beside this beautiful lake. Every year on the same night, a monster emerges from the deep cavern in which it dwells below these waters. Every year, it roams the land, devouring men, women, and children for two days. When the monster is no longer hungry, it returns to its cave, where it remains for another year. This year I intend to wait here by the lake for the monster to emerge. It will crawl out of that water tomorrow night, bringing its terrible hunger. I have planned a feast for tomorrow night and have already invited Sarina and her father so they might witness my heroism. However, I like your suggestions and will give them deep consideration. Servants, find excellent accommodations for my two royal guests, Prince Liam and Princess Annabelle!"

Annie and Liam stood as the servants came to usher them away. "Nasheen," said Annie. "Your men took away some things that belong to us. May we please have them back?"

Nasheen stopped with a golden cup halfway to his lips. "All in good time," he said. "After I have won my bride."

CHAPTER 8

THE NEXT MORNING, Annie and Liam had a wonderful time. They ate breakfast while still in bed, which Annie thought was strange at first, but then decided it was something she could easily get used to. While it was still cool out, they went for a walk through the trees, exclaiming over the exotic birds and unusual plants. The two guards who had found them went along, and when Annie almost stepped on a snake, one of the guards chopped its head off with his curved sword before it could bite her.

The day was unbearably hot when they returned to their tent and nibbled fresh fruit and lightly seasoned stew made of vegetables and a tender meat. After they ate, Annie wanted to wade in the lake. They strolled down to the water, hand in hand, with the two guards trailing behind. Annie slipped off her shoes and stepped into the water, hiking up her gown to keep it dry. "The water feels wonderful!" she told Liam, who was hovering at the edge of the lake. "You should try it!"

"I'd rather watch you in case you need rescuing," he told her. "I'm not sure you should do that if there really is a monster in the lake. Don't go any deeper."

"I won't," said Annie. "The possibility that the story about the monster might be true is the only thing keeping me from swimming. What do you suppose Nasheen is doing today? His tent has been awfully quiet."

"He's probably gone to see that girl Sarina," said Liam. "Watch out! I see ripples in the water over there!"

Annie turned to look. "It was probably just a fish. The water is so clear that you can see them swimming."

"I'd feel a lot better if you'd get out of the lake," Liam told her.

Annie sighed. "Then I will. I don't want to make you worry. You know, this would be a lovely visit if I didn't feel as if we're prisoners." She glanced at the two men who had been with them all day. One of them was watching the water. The other was watching Liam.

"What do you want to do next?" asked Liam.

"Take a nap? It's too hot out here. I feel as if my brains are cooking."

"That sounds good to me," said Liam. "The nap part. Not the cooked brains."

Dragonflies zigzagged over the surface of the water, their greens and blues bright in the hot sun.

Annie retrieved her shoes and slipped them on before hurrying back to the tent and away from prying eyes. She had wanted to talk to Liam, but the heat made them both drowsy and they fell asleep on the bed. They slept through Prince Nasheen's return and the jingling of the bells on his harness as he passed by their tent. They slept through the arrival of the merchant and his daughter, whose escort included twice as many guards and servants as the prince commanded. However, when a musician began to strum his lute in Prince Nasheen's tent, Annie rolled over and sat up.

Liam was still asleep when she crawled off the bed and went to look out the door. Feeling damp and sticky, she wanted nothing more than to wade in the lake again, and splash some water on her face and arms. After debating whether she should wake Liam or let him rest, she left him undisturbed. She knew that one of the guards was following her when she passed between the tents to the water's edge, but she didn't mind. He had already dispatched a snake that day. If the monster showed up early, maybe he could handle that, too.

Annie didn't go far once she reached the water. She was still in sight of the tents when she took off her shoes and waded in just as she had that morning. Holding the bottom of her gown bunched in one hand, she was bending over to scoop water onto her face with the other when she heard splashing behind her. Thinking that the guard had decided to cool off as well, she turned to say something, but the words died on her lips when she saw a lovely girl her own age entering the water.

"Hello," said Annie.

The girl looked up, surprised. "You are a stranger! How odd. I did not expect to find someone from another land here."

Annie smiled. "I'm a little surprised myself. You must be Sarina. My name is Annie. I'm here with—"

"If you are Nasheen's lady friend, you need not tell me. I don't care one way or another. The prince's business is his own until he and my father come to an understanding. At that time, all of Nasheen's business *is* my concern. I came outside so they could negotiate in private. When I saw you, I came to tell you to pack your things and prepare to leave at once."

"I'm not Nasheen's girlfriend!" said Annie. "We don't even like each other! I'm here with my husband and we don't intend to stay long."

Sarina gave Annie a scornful look. "There is no need to make up lies. Nasheen is a most desirable man and the crown prince of Viramoot. Any girl would be happy to marry him. As you can see, he has chosen me, not you!"

"Annie, is everything all right?" Liam called from the shore. He was rumpled from sleep and his hair needed brushing, but Annie thought he was the hand-somest man she knew.

"Just fine," Annie told him. "I was telling Sarina that you and I are on a grand tour, after getting married just a few days ago. Prince Nasheen is an acquaintance of ours, nothing more."

"This man is your husband?" said Sarina.

Annie smiled. It would be a pleasure to set this girl straight. "This man is Prince Liam, crown prince of Dorinocco, and I am his wife, Princess Annabelle of Treecrest. We met Nasheen when he was trying to win the hand of my friend Princess Snow White. But don't worry, she chose another prince, so Nasheen is still available."

"Her loss is my gain," the girl said, trying to look haughty, but Annie thought she no longer looked quite so sure of herself. "Ah! If you will excuse me, I see my father is looking for me. He and Nasheen must have completed their negotiations."

Annie watched as Sarina waded out of the water. The girl that Nasheen had claimed was a natural beauty had become quite plain while standing near Annie. And apparently her inability to acknowledge him had been a ploy. She certainly seemed eager to accept his proposal now.

"I came to tell you that it's time to get ready for sup-per," Liam said as Annie waded toward him. "They say we're eating early so Nasheen will be ready to fight the monster."

"Have I told you how much I love you?" Annie asked, putting her arms around his neck.

"Not in the last few minutes," he told her, holding her even closer.

They were sharing a kiss when the guard who had followed Liam cleared his throat loud enough to get their attention. He didn't say anything, but his glance to the group of tents was enough. Seeing the flurry of activity in front of Nasheen's tent made them hurry off the beach and back to the tent they were using.

Annie and Liam cleaned up as best they could without a change of clothes and were ready to go a short time later. When they arrived at Nasheen's tent, they found a group of courtiers that they had never seen before, along with Sarina and her father. Everyone stood until Nasheen arrived, and then Sarina and her father were seated beside him. Annie and Liam found themselves seated at the far end of the table, which didn't bother Annie at all.

The food was brought out one course after another. Most of the dishes were so exotic that Annie didn't recognize them. Some were so heavily spiced that she couldn't eat them, and one was so hot that her mouth burned no matter what she ate or drank after that. Liam was able to eat more than she did, but neither of them ate very much. Prince Nasheen and the merchant, however, seemed to eat more than anyone.

They had just finished a dessert of a lumpy liquid that was cool and sweet when Nasheen stood up. Everyone stopped talking and looked his way. "I have an announcement to make!" he said. "The lovely Sarina and I are to be wed in one month's time. In exchange for her hand, I have agreed to give her father fifty goats, twenty horses, and a chest of gold that weighs as much as my new bride. I have also promised him an exalted position in my court."

While the others called out their congratulations to the engaged couple, Annie and Liam exchanged glances. Nasheen had gotten his bride, but would he say that Annie had helped and let them go, or claim he had done it on his own and lock them away forever? Neither of them thought very highly of the prince or his promises.

When the meal was over and everyone was leaving the table, Annie pushed past the last of the well-wishers to confront Nasheen. "You said that you would give our things back to us and let us go once Sarina accepted your proposal. May we have our possessions back now?"

"I said that I would give you back your trinkets, but I never said that I would let you go," said Nasheen. "Guards!

Return them to their tent and keep them there until my arrival. I will reveal their future to them then."

"I am so glad Snow White didn't choose him," Annie told Liam as the guards hustled them between the tents. "He would have made her an awful husband, but I think he's perfect for Sarina!"

Annie hoped the guards were taking them back to the tent they had just left, but she knew as soon as they turned a different way that they were going to the small, dark tent where she and Liam had first waited for Nasheen. Even before they reached the little tent, servants began to pack up the rest, loading them onto wagons. Annie and Liam sat in the tent listening to wheels creaking and men shouting, wondering what Nasheen had planned.

When the prince finally arrived, he had a lantern and more guards with him. While two guards held their swords aimed at Annie and Liam, two others fastened shackles on their wrists and ankles. "I have been told that the monster would be satisfied with royal blood and not seek any other until the next year, but the theory has never been tested until now. Recently, a wizard stopped by to warn me that you two were coming here. He suggested that I use you to sate the monster's hunger. I thought it was an excellent suggestion and was pleased when you actually showed up. That reminds me—I did promise to return your possessions, worthless as they are, and I always keep my promises."

When Nasheen gestured, a guard handed him two bags. The prince dumped the contents of one bag on the ground beside Liam. Annie was relieved to see that the postcards were among the jumbled belongings. Before returning Annie's items to her, Nasheen plucked something from the bag, then poured the rest onto the ground.

Nasheen held up the blue stone that the yetis had given to Annie and inspected it closely. "I'm told this is a calming stone that can calm the fiercest beast or most horrible monster. When I saw it, I thought about keeping it for future use, but I think I'll give it to you as a kind of insurance. After the monster eats you, he'll have two people and the calming stone in his belly. If you two aren't enough, the stone should make it less vicious and I will have my men slay it. Either way, I will have killed the monster and become a hero in the eyes of my beloved and my people. To ensure that the monster swallows the stone when it eats you, I think I'll place it somewhere you can't remove it. No need to risk you trying to feed it to the beast in an attempt to save yourselves. This should do just fine," he said, tucking it down the back of Annie's gown.

"I will be leaving soon, so it is time I said farewell. I hope you both have a pleasant evening!" he said. A moment later, he was out of the tent, taking the lantern with him, and the guards were fastening the flap closed behind him.

"I'm surprised," said Annie. "Nasheen is even more despicable than I thought he was."

"I'm not surprised," Liam replied. "I never liked him. I have to say, though, it looks like Rotan really got around."

"Nasheen didn't give us back our coats, but at least we have the cards," said Annie.

Liam bumped into her, and immediately moved away. She could hear him shifting around beside her. "If you come toward me and roll onto your side, you should be able to pick up your things. I've almost collected my postcards."

Annie did as he suggested and had picked up everything, including the doll and the ring, when the stomp of something heavy shook the little tent. "Hurry!" she told Liam. "That must be the monster."

"Just a moment," said Liam. "I think there's one more postcard. I can reach it with my fingertips."

"We don't have a moment!" Annie cried, fear making her voice rise as the heavy footsteps drew closer. "It's almost here!"

"There! I got the last one," said Liam. "Give me your hand. I don't know which card is on top, but it doesn't matter now. Any of them should be better than this."

The footsteps stopped just outside the tent. Suddenly Annie heard scraping as claws pierced the tent wall. She screamed as the wall was ripped to shreds.

"Annie, your hand!" Liam shouted. And they were gone.

CHAPTER 9

"WELL," SAID ANNIE. "At least it isn't a desert!"

"But there's still sand," Liam grumbled. "I'm getting really tired of sand!"

They were seated on a beach at the edge of a large body of water. Annie spotted a few small islands a distance away, but there were no boats or people around. When she looked behind her, she saw that the beach was edged with plants like the odd ones they had seen in Viramoot. She could hear birds, but their voices were harsher than the birds at home. "Either we're still in Viramoot, or those trees aren't that uncommon," she said. "What should we do now? We have to get these shackles off."

"I don't have anything we can use," said Liam. "We can search the shoreline and see if we can find something useful, or go inland and hope we meet someone who can help us."

"After running into Nasheen, I'm not so sure that's a good idea. Rotan might have told lies about us to people at all the rest of the places pictured on the postcards. Maybe avoiding people would be a better idea now."

"Fine with me," Liam said as he got to his feet. "The shackles won't let us take normal steps, but we can walk with them on." He took Annie's hand and helped her up, steadying her as she got her balance.

They walked along the shore, looking for something hard they could use to pound the shackles to break them, or even pry them open. Shuffling with the shackles' heavy weights on her ankles wasn't easy, but Annie got used to it after a while. "We weren't there for the monster to eat," she finally said, "which meant it had to look for another meal. How far do you think Nasheen and his men got before the monster went after them?"

Liam chuckled. "Not far! From what I know of Nasheen, he probably stopped to hear the monster eat us."

"Poor Sarina! She'll be so disappointed if she doesn't get to marry a prince," said Annie.

"I think her father would be even more disappointed," Liam told her. "I was watching his face when Nasheen made his announcement. That merchant couldn't wait to get his hands on all that gold and take on his new position at court."

"He sounds like Rotan. Both of them want high positions at court," said Annie.

"That's true," said Liam. "The big difference between them is how they go about getting one. Sarina's father is going to marry his daughter off for a position in Nasheen's court, while Rotan wants to get us killed for a place in Clarence's."

Annie sighed. "This trip would be much more fun if people weren't trying to kill us." She paused mid-step to listen. "I hear something. Do you think that's thunder?"

Liam cocked his head to the side. "That rumbling sound? Maybe. I think—"

A tree cracked farther inland. Annie and Liam could see the top of the tree waver and fall, crashing to the ground. The birdsong had stopped with the first crack, and now the only sound was that of the waves rolling to the shore. Other trees near the one that had fallen thrashed back and forth long after the first one fell, but they all remained upright. Annie glanced at Liam as the ground shook as if something big was headed their way, but then it stopped and the birdsong started again.

"I don't think I want to go inland if we can help it," said Annie. "I'm not sure I want to know what's moving around in there."

"Too bad this entire beach is covered with fine, white sand. A good solid rock would come in handy right now."

Annie sighed. "This is beautiful, though. If I'd seen this postcard first, I might even have chosen to come here. This is our grand tour, after all. We're supposed to be having fun. Look over there! I've never seen turquoise water before. And do you see how shallow it looks even way out there? I wish we could go swimming while we're here."

"Maybe we can, if we can get these shackles off. And if there aren't any monsters around. And if we don't have to leave suddenly because something awful is about to befall us if we stay here," said Liam.

Annie glanced at the trees again. "It looks calm now. Let's hope it stays that way."

They continued walking, rounding the curve in the beach. When they reached the far side of the curve, they discovered an outcropping of rocks that led out into the water. Liam was delighted to find smaller rocks at the base of the boulders and searched until he found just the right one. Perched on one of the larger rocks, he stretched the chain between his ankles across the hard surface, and pounded it with the smaller rock. A few minutes of pounding broke the chains. When he gestured to Annie, she sat down and stuck her fingers in her ears while he tried to break the chain between her ankles.

Liam was still focused on Annie's chains when a shadow fell across the rocks and a sweet voice boomed, "Watcha doing?"

Even with Annie's fingers in her ears, the voice was painfully loud. Annie looked up and saw a young girl, no more than six years old, towering above her. She was very pretty, with dark brown curls and sky-blue eyes, but she was at least three times taller than Liam when he was standing. *The girl must be a giant!* Annie thought. She had never seen a giant before, and had never believed they were real, but confronted with such a big little girl, she couldn't imagine what else the child might be.

A drop of water landed on Annie's head and ran down her cheek. The girl was clutching a bouquet of odd-looking flowers that dripped water from their petals.

Annie scooted backward, trying to get away from the dripping flowers. When she glanced at Liam, his eyes were as big as saucers and his mouth was hanging open. Apparently, it was going to be up to her to talk to the girl. "We're trying to break these chains," said Annie, answering her question.

"Why?" asked the girl.

"Because we don't want them on anymore," said Annie.

"Why?"

"Because they make it hard to walk."

"Why?"

Annie decided that it was time to take charge of the conversation. "You have some interesting flowers," she told the girl.

"They aren't mine," the girl replied. "They're Blooger's. He lets me play with them."

"I probably shouldn't ask this, but who is Blooger?"

"He's my friend," the girl said, holding the bouquet toward Annie and turning around. "See? That's him right there."

A large, sand-colored mass drooped down the girl's back and spread out just below the surface of the water behind her. Annie thought it wasn't alive until she saw it undulating against the wash of waves as it worked to stay where it was and not get swept away. It blended into the sand below it, with only the garden of waving "flowers" attached to its back standing out. Suddenly Annie realized that the flowers clutched in the girl's hands weren't flowers at all, but growths that were part of a sea monster.

Startled, Annie cried out. The sound seemed to bring Liam out of his stupor. Shouting, "I'll save you!" he jumped off the rock and lunged toward the monster, holding the rock in one hand. He tried to hit the monster, but the creature was so squishy that the rock didn't do any damage. It did seem to frighten the monster, however, because it made a soft mewling sound, pulled all its "flowers" out of the girl's grasp, and fled into deeper water.

The girl wailed and started to cry in great heaving sobs that made Annie clap her hands over her ears again. There was a loud roar and another monster swimming in the deeper water roared and came racing toward them even as the first one turned and started back. Water frothed behind the new monster and Annie could just make out its long, whiplike tail that propelled it through the waves at great speed.

"Annie, quick! Get out of the water!" Liam shouted. Wading toward her, he put his hands on her waist and lifted her onto the rocks before turning to face the advancing monsters.

"What's going on here?" shouted a voice so loud that Annie's ears rang with the sound of it. Turning toward the forest, she saw more giants emerge from among the trees. The tallest, who would have looked like an ordinary man if he hadn't been more than forty feet tall, was so similar to the little girl that he had to be her father. Annie assumed that the giant woman running beside him was the child's mother. They had just reached the edge of the water when two boys came racing down the beach. With every step that the giants took, the earth shook beneath their feet, making it lurch and bounce beneath Annie and Liam.

"It's a family of giants!" Annie said out loud, but her ears were still ringing and she couldn't hear her own voice.

She turned to Liam to see if he knew, but he was facing the two sea monsters with nothing more than a rock in his hand. Without a sword, he was virtually defenseless.

"Penelope!" the giant woman cried, lumbering into the water and scooping up the girl. "What's wrong?"

"Blooger went away and took my flowers!" the giant girl sobbed.

"We've talked about this before," her mother told Penelope while drying the child's tears. "Those are Blooger's flowers. It's very nice of him to let you play with them, but you have to give them back when he leaves."

"Mona, I believe that Penelope has made some new friends," the girl's father said, lowering his voice. Annie turned away from the crying child and found the giant looking from her to Liam. "It seems some wee ones have arrived on our little paradise. Young man, you don't need to defend Penelope from the sea monsters anymore. They are actually her babysitters and are here to protect her. Blooger, Squidge, thank you for watching over Penelope today. Her mother and I can take over now."

Liam didn't back away until both monsters turned and swam off. Annie sighed with relief. Liam was the bravest man she knew, but that didn't mean he couldn't get hurt.

"More wee ones?" said Mona. "So many visitors in such a short time."

"Papa, what's going on?" one of the boys asked, eyeing Liam, who was still holding the rock.

"Just a misunderstanding," said his father. "We seem to have some new arrivals. What's this? Why are you wearing chains? Are you escaped criminals?"

"Nothing like that!" Liam replied. "A false friend shackled us and left us for a monster to eat. We escaped through magic and came here. I was trying to remove the shackles when your daughter found us."

"Ah!" said the father. "Perhaps one of my sons can help you. Their hands are smaller than mine and can handle delicate things like your shackles. Clifton, why don't you see what you can do?"

"I'm not sure that's a good idea," Liam said as the two boys approached. They were both over thirty feet tall, although they looked like they were in their early teens.

"I've got this," said the bigger boy.

When he squatted down and reached for the shackles, Annie could tell that Liam was fighting the urge to pull away. The boy was surprisingly gentle, however. Jamming his fingernail into the gap in the shackles, he pried them apart one at a time. When he had removed Liam's shackles, he turned to Annie's. His hands were enormous, but he was so careful that she barely felt any extra pressure as the shackles came off.

Liam turned to Mona, the mother giant. "You said 'more wee ones.' Have others been here recently?"

"Only one," said Mona. "It was an old man in long robes with a shiny head. He saw us and ran away laughing. He must have left the island then, because we never saw him again."

"Rotan!" Annie exclaimed. "He's a nasty wizard who does nothing but cause trouble. Liam and I just got married and are on our grand tour. Somehow Rotan knows where we're going and has gone ahead to turn people against us."

"Then I'm glad he didn't stay," said the father giant. "You, however, are welcome to stay as long as you like. My name is Hugo and this island belongs to my family and me."

"We'd love to stay for a little while," Annie said, casting a glance at Liam. "I think we could both use a good rest."

CHAPTER 10

AFTER ANNIE AND Liam agreed to stay, the family of giants returned home, taking Penelope with them. Annie and Liam were left alone on the beach, which Annie thought was perfect.

"The shackles are off, the monsters are gone, and nothing dire is making us leave. Can we go for a swim now?" Annie asked Liam.

"I don't know why not," Liam said as he pulled his shirt off over his head.

When Annie took off her gown, she was careful to retrieve the blue stone that Nasheen had dropped down her back. Tucking it in her pocket with the rest of the gifts from the yetis, she folded the gown and set it above the tide's reach.

Annie and Liam went swimming in their undergarments, laughing as they splashed each other, then swimming together in lazy circles. Suddenly Liam disappeared. A moment later, Annie felt a hand on her ankle and something jerked her under the water. She was relieved to see that it was Liam, and moved into his arms without protest. They kissed for as long as they could both hold their breath, then shot to the surface, laughing.

"You know," Annie said after a while. "So far, this is the only part of our trip that's anything like the way I envisioned our grand tour. I thought we'd spend long, lazy days relaxing and enjoying each other's company, but it's all been so hectic, and sometimes quite frightening!"

"I know it didn't turn out at all as we'd planned," said Liam. "I am sorry; I know it's my fault."

"Don't you dare feel bad," Annie told him. "This is just another of our adventures! Only, I do wish we knew that there was a way for us to get home in the end."

"I swear to you, Annie," Liam said, reaching for her hand. "I will find a way to get us home, even if it takes me years and years and—"

"Oh, you!" she said, laughing as she splashed him, starting yet another water battle.

ॐ

They were floating on their backs, holding hands while watching the high white clouds drifting overhead, when Annie said, "The giants are so nice! The stories about them always make them out to be fierce and nasty, but they aren't at all."

"Maybe some are, but this family is very nice," said Liam.

"Hugo seemed to accept everything you said without question. Why do you think that is?"

"I don't know," Liam replied. "Maybe giants don't lie and aren't used to people who do. Or maybe we're so small and insignificant to them that we're not a threat no matter what."

"I suppose either could be true. Speaking of liars, why do you think Rotan ran away laughing when he saw the giants?"

"Considering how he's trying to turn people against us, maybe he saw the giants and thought he didn't need to say anything. Maybe he thought they were so dangerous that we wouldn't survive a visit here," said Liam.

"I bet you're right," Annie replied. "I know I said that I wanted to go places we'd never visited before, and we've definitely done that. We've seen so many interesting places and met so many fascinating people that I think my desire to travel has been satisfied. Speaking of new people, do you think the giants might be able to help us find our way home?"

"We can ask, but I doubt it. I didn't know giants were real, any more than I knew fire-breathing dragons were real. I wouldn't be surprised if we're as far from home here as we were in East Aridia. Please don't worry. I'm sure we'll find a way home sooner or later."

Annie glanced at him and nodded. Knowing that Rotan was working against them and that they didn't have a postcard to take them home worried Annie more than she'd let on. Although she was the only one to bring it up, she had a feeling that Liam was just as concerned. Reminding him of it wasn't going to help matters. The best thing she could do was keep her eyes open and remember that Liam was also looking for a way home.

Seeing the troubled look in Liam's eyes, Annie decided that it was time to talk about something else. "When we get home, what do you think we should do about your mother and Clarence? Have you come up with anything yet?"

Liam groaned and let his feet drop so that he was standing. "I still don't know. I'd hoped something would occur to me, but everything I come up with is too cruel or wouldn't work, and they'd be back trying to take over the kingdom again. The only thing I know for sure is that I don't want them anywhere near us when we do go home."

The ground started to shake as the two boy giants appeared at the edge of the trees and ran across the sand, tearing off their outer clothes. "Wahoo!" they thundered as they flung themselves into the water.

A wall of water crashed into Annie and Liam, carrying them, with churning feet and flailing arms, down the shore and into deeper water. Annie tumbled over and over, losing track of Liam within the first few seconds. When she finally came up gasping, she saw him farther down the beach, searching the water for her.

"Annie!" he shouted when he spotted her head bobbing above the waves.

The stable boys at the castle had taught Annie how to swim and often jumped in the Crystal River with her on hot summer days. When the snow melted in the mountains, the river's current could be dangerously strong, but Annie had found it exhilarating and enjoyed it even more. Now at the beach, she had found the gentle waves soothing, and a little boring. The giants' wave had disoriented her at first, but it had also been a lot of fun!

"That was great!" she said as she swam toward Liam. She glanced back at the two boys frolicking in deeper water; they seemed oblivious to what they had done.

"Are you all right?" Liam asked Annie as he swam closer.

"I'm fine," she said. "I was just wondering if we could ask them to do it again."

"Really?" said Liam. "I was just wondering how long it's going to take us to find our clothes. That wave washed everything off the stretch of beach where we left them."

"Oh, no! They could be anywhere!" Annie cried.

"Then we'd better start looking," said Liam.

Annie found her gown snagged on the rocks. She was relieved to find that her possessions were still tucked inside the pocket. It didn't take her long to find Liam's shoes and one of her own, but after hours of looking, Liam's shirt was still missing and so was her other shoe. Late that afternoon, they were standing on the shore, about to give up, when Liam spotted the sea monster named Squidge swimming toward them.

"Did you lose something?" Squidge asked in a gurgling voice.

"A couple of things, actually," said Liam.

"Then these might be yours," the monster said, and used his long tail to toss the shirt and the shoe onto the beach.

"Thank you!" Annie called after the retreating monster. "That was very nice of him," she told Liam.

"It might have been nicer if my shirt didn't look like someone had gnawed a hole in it," grumbled Liam.

They were spreading his shirt on the sand to dry alongside the other wet clothes when Penelope's father trudged onto the beach. Crouching down beside them, he whispered in a voice that was still loud to Annie and Liam. "My wife sent me to invite you to supper. I hope you like fish."

"That sounds wonderful," said Annie. "Thank you for inviting us."

"We had to," whispered the giant. "Penelope hasn't stopped talking about you. Supper should be ready in an hour."

"We'll be there," said Liam.

The giant was already walking away when Annie said, "We forgot to ask him where we should go."

"That's easy," said Liam. "We'll follow the path." He pointed at the ground where the giant had been standing. It was at least two feet lower than the ground under the trees. Finding the giants shouldn't be difficult.

❦

The path that the giants had trod into the forest floor was as easy to follow as a king's road. Annie and Liam would have reached the cottage in no time if there hadn't been so many interesting things to see on the way. The giants had obviously been busy making the island their home. They had planted gardens on both sides of the path, growing melons as big as cottages, squash longer than Liam was tall, carrots with feathery tops that grew as high as the trees, and green beans that would have made wonderful boats for humans.

When Annie and Liam heard the sound of scraping ahead, they thought they would find a member of Hugo's family, but instead they came across a high fence with a small flock of chickens as big as normal cows scratching at the ground and clucking softly to themselves. One of the chickens stopped to tilt its head to the side and eye them, which made Annie and Liam hurry past. They laughed when the chickens didn't follow them and they saw the relief on each other's faces.

Liam was the first to stop and sniff the air. "I can smell fish cooking," he said. "It smells wonderful!"

"We haven't eaten in a while," said Annie. "It does smell good. I think they're cooking onions and garlic, too."

"Do you think you could walk a little faster?" said Liam. "Suddenly, I'm really hungry!"

A few minutes later the cottage came into sight. The building was only one floor high, but it had to be at least fifty feet tall. The windows were all open, letting a cool breeze wash through. A wide front door painted red stood open as well, and Annie could see someone moving around inside the cottage.

"Should we knock or call out or what?" Annie asked as they approached the door.

"I think we should shout as loud as we can," said Liam. "And even then I doubt they'll hear us."

Fortunately, they didn't need to do either, because Penelope was there, watching for them. Liam had given Annie a hand to pull her onto the threshold when the child cried out, "They're here, Mommy! They came for supper!"

Annie let go of Liam and clapped her hands to her ears to block the child's loud voice. Even so, her ears rang as she stepped into the cottage and looked around. They were in the kitchen and the aroma of cooking food was almost overwhelming. Annie couldn't see much other than the underside of an enormous table and part of the fireplace that was as big as a normal-size cottage. Steam rose from food already on the table, while something boiled in a pot still hanging from a hook in the fireplace. Annie and Liam stepped back as Mona strode past them, moving something from one side of the table to the other, her long skirts swirling around her ankles, creating a breeze as she walked. Penelope sat in a chair pushed up to the table, watching as avidly as a cat might watch a mouse.

"Penelope, why don't you help our guests to their place at the table?" said her mother. "I'm just about to call your brothers to supper, and the wee ones would be safer if they were already seated."

Annie looked up as the girl climbed down from her chair to loom over them. Before she knew what was happening, Annie was cupped in the Penelope's hand, whooshing through the air to a huge wooden plate on the table. The girl set her on the plate, plunking Liam beside her a moment later.

"Well, that was different!" Liam said, sounding slightly out of breath.

"At least she was gentle," Annie whispered to him as Penelope took her place at the table again. Her plate was beside the one where Annie and Liam were sitting, although the space between them was wider than a jousting field.

Annie was startled when Mona began to ring a bell. The sound was as loud as if Annie had been inside it, hanging on to the clapper. Her head was throbbing when the bell stopped ringing. A minute later, the two boys and their father stomped into the kitchen and took their places at the table.

"Good! I see our guests are here," said Hugo in his normal voice.

Annie winced and covered her ears.

"Oh, sorry," Hugo whispered when he saw her. "Remember, everyone, soft voices. Our guests can't handle loud noises."

"Why?" asked Penelope, peering down at Annie and Liam.

"Because they're small and fragile," Clifton said from where he sat on the other side of his sister. He ruffled her hair and she laughed, a light, joyous sound that Annie would have thought delightful if it hadn't been so loud.

"Supper looks delicious!" Hugo told Mona, beaming down the length of the table at her. "Pass your plates, everyone! Let's eat before supper gets cold. Uh, you two might want to get off before I serve your dinner."

The entire family watched as Liam helped Annie down from the plate, and stepped aside as Hugo reached for it. They couldn't see what was in the bowls or what he put on the plate until he set it back on the table with a thud that nearly knocked them off their feet. Annie was peering over the edge, wondering how they were supposed to reach the food, when Penelope picked them up and set them back on the plate.

"Eat your supper!" she ordered them, remembering to keep her voice down.

Annie glanced at Liam. They had no utensils and doubted that the giants had any the right size for them anyway. "I guess we have to use our hands."

Liam shrugged. "It's no worse than when we camp out," he said. "I wonder what kind of fish that is."

Annie stood up to see what was on the plate. The big slab of something white covered in garlic and onions had to be the fish. Sliced carrots as big around as a barrel lid rested beside a huge mound of mashed turnips. On the far side of the plate, a puddle of something soft and squishy could have been some kind of pudding. Although the servings might be small by a giant's standards, there was far too much food for two "wee ones."

As the giants began to eat, Annie and Liam stepped closer to the food. Annie tasted a sliver of fish so big that she had to use both hands to hold it. After the first bite, she had to admit that it was delicious. She was very careful as she ate her food, tearing off small pieces of fish or tiny chunks of carrots, but Liam was more forthright in the way he ate. After tasting the fish and carrots, he moved on to the turnips, eating a sizable hole in the mound before Annie had tried any. When she looked at him again, he was eating pudding, digging his hands into it and scooping it out by the fistful.

"Hasn't anyone ever told you not to play with your food?" Annie said with a laugh.

"This is really good!" said Liam. "There are bits of fruit in it that I've never tasted before."

Annie smiled even as she shook her head. He had pudding smeared up to his elbows, but he really did seem to like it. She was about to taste the pudding herself, when Penelope said to Annie and Liam, "How come you're so little?"

Annie glanced at Liam to see if he was going to answer, but he was engrossed in the mashed turnips again and didn't seem to have noticed that Penelope was talking to them. "All humans are little like us. It's just the way we're made," Annie finally told her.

"Will you get any bigger?"

"This is probably about as big as we'll get. We might grow a little more, but we'll never be as big as you."

"How can you walk on such little feet? Don't you fall over a lot? I know I would if my feet were as little as yours."

"Our feet are the right size for our bodies. We don't fall over any more than you do."

"Where do you come from?"

Although the other giants hadn't seemed to be interested in the conversation before this, talking among themselves and eating loudly, they all grew quiet now. "I come from a kingdom called Treecrest. Liam is from Dorinocco. Do you know where either of those kingdoms are located?" she said, turning to Hugo.

Hugo shook his head. Apparently he had been listening. "I've never heard of them. We used to live in Upper Montevista and have friends who live in Greater Greensward. And we passed through Soggy Molvinia, remember, Mona?"

"I remember that, I just don't remember hearing of any place named Treecrest or Dorinocco."

"And we've never heard of the kingdoms you mentioned," said Liam, who must have been listening as well.

Annie shot him a quick glance. They may not have heard of any Montevista or Molvinia, but they had heard of Greater Greensward, and what they'd heard hadn't been good. Apparently the giants weren't going to be able to help them, either.

⁊

It was getting dark by the time they finished eating, and it occurred to Annie that they had nowhere to spend the night. "I suppose we could sleep on the beach," she told Liam.

"I don't know how safe that would be," he said. "We don't know what kind of wild animals live on this island."

"You could sleep here," said Penelope. "Couldn't they, Mama? They could sleep in Lulu's bed. She wouldn't mind."

"That's a good idea," her mother replied. "Why don't you show it to them and see what they think?"

"Lulu's bed is next to mine," Penelope said as she got down from her chair. "Come on. I'll show you."

Who is Lulu? Annie wondered, but before she could ask, Penelope had picked her up again. "Oof!" said Annie. She wished the child weren't so eager to carry her around. In her excitement, Penelope wasn't as gentle as she'd been before, and Annie was finding it hard to breathe. She pushed on the girl's fingers, trying to get more space, but it didn't make any difference. Gasping for air, Annie didn't notice that they were in a different room until Penelope set her on the floor.

"Will you be my friend?" asked Penelope.

Annie drew in a deep breath, despite her now sore ribs. "I'd be happy to be your friend," she replied, and coughed from the effort, making her ribs hurt more.

"Good! Then you can stay here forever and I'll take good care of you. See, this is Lulu's bed. Lulu, time to get up!"

A bed the right size for a human sat on the floor beside an enormous bed that was obviously Penelope's. Annie was horrified when the child pulled back the covers on the little bed and picked up a person who seemed to be as rigid as a board.

"My brother made Lulu for me when I was little," said Penelope. "She can sleep in my bed with me from now on and you can sleep in this bed."

Lulu is a doll, Annie realized. And Penelope wanted Annie to take her place! "Uh, Penelope," Annie began. "Liam and I are going to be here only a day or two. We can't stay here forever!"

"Oh! I forgot Liam! Here, you get in bed and I'll go get him," Penelope said, picking Annie up and setting her on the bed. "Lie down and I'll cover you up."

"I don't think . . . ," Annie began, but she choked on her next words when Penelope pushed her down with one massive finger and pulled the covers over her.

"I'll be right back," said the girl, leaving Annie to rub her chest where the girl had poked her.

Annie lay there, listening to the giant child walk away. She was about to sit up when she heard Penelope returning. After waiting for the girl to set Liam on the bed, she watched her tuck him under the covers.

"I have to get ready for bed now," said Penelope. "I'll check on you when I get in my bed."

Annie waited while the girl left the room and she was alone with Liam before speaking. "Penelope's treating us like dolls," she told him. "This is a doll's bed. She said that we can use it forever."

"Apparently you're her favorite doll. She told me that she would throw me in the ocean if I wasn't nice to you," said Liam.

Annie shuddered. "We can't stay here! We have to leave tonight."

"We will as soon as she goes to sleep," agreed Liam. "It's too bad. I would have liked to spend another day on the beach with you."

"I'd like that, too, just not here," said Annie. "Now I can't stop worrying that she's going to pitch you into the water the first time we argue."

"Are you two comfy?" Penelope said as she came back in the room. "You should be asleep already. Close your eyes and go to sleep right now!"

Annie closed her eyes immediately, hoping that Liam had done the same. She lay there, pretending to be asleep, while Penelope climbed into bed. When Mona and Hugo came in to kiss their daughter good night, Annie didn't budge. Even after they blew out the candle, and the room was dark, she kept her eyes closed and her breathing regular. It worked so well, and she was so tired, that she fell asleep when she fully intended to stay awake.

Liam must have fallen asleep, too, because when Annie woke a few hours later, he was snoring softly beside her. Scooting closer to him, she whispered, "Liam, wake up!"

"Huh? What? I wasn't asleep! I was just resting my eyes," he said in a normal voice.

"Shh!" Annie whispered back as she poked him in the side. "Quiet! You don't want to wake Penelope!"

"Mmm," the girl murmured. "What's wrong? Why are you talking? Go back to sleep."

Even though the giant child couldn't see her, Annie closed her eyes again and pretended to sleep. This time she managed to stay awake. When Penelope's breathing evened out, Annie nudged Liam and was relieved when he patted her hand without talking. Moving as quietly as they could, they edged off the bed and tiptoed from the room.

To Annie's surprise, Hugo was sitting on a bench by the fireplace, gazing into the flames. "Leaving, are you?" he asked when he saw them. "I don't blame you. Penelope can be a little bossy."

"She's a sweet child, but she's treating us like dolls," said Annie. "Please tell her that we had to go."

127

"I will," Hugo murmured. "She'll be disappointed, but it can't be helped. Good luck with your travels. I'm glad we got to meet you. It was a nice diversion. Life here is very pleasant, but it can get a bit boring."

"After all the excitement Annie and I have lived through lately, I'm looking forward to a little boring time of my own," said Liam. "Thank you for your hospitality."

"It was my pleasure!" said the giant, smiling in the near darkness.

CHAPTER 11

"YOU SAID YOU'D like to spend more time with me on a beach," Annie said to Liam. "It looks as if you got your wish."

"I know," said Liam. "But we won't know if we can relax until we find out who or what lives here."

The next postcard had been a picture of a beautiful tropical island. It looked a lot like the island where the giants lived, only smaller and with shorter, more windswept trees. Although it was dawn and the sky was just starting to lighten, Annie could see well enough to decide that the white sand beaches looked as inviting as those on the other island. Even so, she wasn't sure that she and Liam dared go swimming.

"The first thing we need to do is explore," Liam announced. "I'm tired of surprises. Let's see what lies inland before we check the shoreline."

They started toward the center of the island, their feet sinking into sand still cool from the night. When they reached the first of the trees, they disturbed a flock of brightly colored birds that flew away squawking, their long tails hanging down behind them. The day was starting to get warm when Annie spotted the glint of sunlight on water. She hurried ahead, hoping to find fresh water that they could drink. To her delight she found a medium-size pond filled with cool, clear water.

"Do you think we can drink it?" she asked as Liam caught up with her.

"Don't run ahead like that!" Liam told her. "How am I supposed to protect you if I don't go first? Wait a minute while I check the water. I don't want you drinking anything until I know it's all right."

Liam knelt beside the pond and scooped up a small amount of water. He sniffed it first, then stuck his tongue in for the tiniest taste. The next sip he took was larger. He held it in his mouth for a moment before swallowing it.

"Well?" said Annie. "How is it?"

"It tastes wonderful, but we really should wait to see if I get sick before . . . Annie, don't!"

Annie was on her knees, scooping up water and taking a long, cool sip before Liam could finish his sentence. When she'd finished, she sat back and turned to Liam. "If you're going to get sick, so am I. Oh my, look at your shirt! What did you do, take a bath in that pudding last night?"

"There weren't any spoons!" he replied, glancing down at himself. He patted his chest where the fabric was stiff and still sticky. "I must admit, this is disgusting, and very uncomfortable."

"Take that shirt off and let me rinse it out for you," Annie told him. "I don't have any soap, but rinsing it should make it a little more wearable."

Liam grumbled as he slipped off his shirt. Taking the postcards from his pocket, he set them on the ground and handed the shirt to Annie. While she scrubbed the shirt under water, Liam rinsed off his arms and upper body. They were leaning over the water, intent on their tasks, when they heard voices coming through the trees. Two elderly women wearing strange loose gowns made of red, yellow, and orange fabric stopped at the edge of the trees to stare at them. While the short, plump woman had a kindly look about her, the stick-thin woman wore a sour expression on her long face, crinkling her narrow nose as if she saw something repulsive.

"Well, I'll be! What have we here?" said the shorter woman.

"They're the two intruders come to steal our treasure, Norelle," said the other. "I guess that old geezer was right after all."

Annie stood up and handed Liam's shirt back to him while saying, "Please pardon us. We aren't thieves, nor did we mean to intrude. We can leave now if you don't want us here."

"Leave? Who said anything about leaving?" snapped the taller woman. "Come with us so you can meet the rest of the ladies."

Annie bent down to brush a leaf from her foot, moving so the two women couldn't see her pick up the postcards. When she stood, she kept her hand behind her and tucked the cards into one of her pockets, hoping no one had noticed.

"Come along!" ordered the taller woman, and walked away without waiting for Annie and Liam to follow.

Norelle gave Annie an encouraging smile before scurrying off after her friend.

"I guess we found the people who live here," Liam said as they started to follow. "That woman said we should meet the ladies. Do you suppose they're *all* women?"

"We'll know soon enough," said Annie. "I see some buildings up ahead."

Liam grunted as they stepped out of the trees onto the beach. It was on the opposite side of the island from where they'd arrived and looked very different, with a cluster of huts and a large fire pit edged with driftwood. "This island is smaller than I thought," he muttered.

"The old wizard was right," the taller woman shouted. "They're here!"

"Thank you, Rugene. We can see that," said a woman with long white hair, her voice surprisingly husky. "Now we have to decide what we're going to do about it."

"I think we should do what he said," declared another woman. Her gray hair looked as if it had never been brushed and her gown was grimy and torn. Annie noticed that the others gave her wary looks and kept their distance from her.

"I'm not doing anything that nincompoop said!" said Rugene. "He didn't ask us, he ordered us to tie them up and toss them in the ocean, as if he has any right to tell us what to do! I may not be using my magic much lately, but I still have more magic in my little toe than he has in his big, bald head!"

"They're witches!" Annie whispered in Liam's ear.

"And Rotan has been here," Liam whispered back. "May I say something?" he asked the witches.

"NO!" they all shouted at once.

"This is up to us, not you," Rugene told him. "So keep your mouth shut if you know what's good for you!"

"I think we should vote like we usually do," said Norelle. "I vote we give them breakfast and send them on their way."

"Give them breakfast! Next you'll be inviting them to move in!" cried the witch with the wild hair.

"They look a bit thin, Hennah, that's all," said Norelle.

"I'm not so sure about breakfast, but I didn't sleep well last night and I don't feel up to drowning anyone today," the witch with long white hair announced. "And that old wizard was so rude. I agree with Norelle. I think we should send them away."

A witch with sad-looking eyes wrung her hands, saying, "Cadmilla is right. No breakfast, and send them away. They may be thieves, but that doesn't mean they deserve to drown. No one has stolen anything from us yet. And we've all stolen something in the past, some more than others, but nobody tried to drown us."

"Speak for yourself, Septicimia!" said Hennah. "I've been tossed in more lakes and ponds than I can remember. One old coot tried to drown me in a cesspool!"

"Not that we ever had treasure for anyone to steal," said Cadmilla. "I wonder why the wizard thought we did."

"Back to the vote," Norelle declared. "Who hasn't voted yet?"

When the last two witches voted against tossing them into the ocean, Annie gave Liam a look of relief.

"I don't agree," said Hennah. Raising her arm, she pointed at Annie and Liam. Annie grabbed Liam's hand and held on tight. The old witch muttered something under her breath, and a sickly green light shot from her fingertip, hit Annie and Liam, and bounced back. The light slammed into the witch with such force that it knocked her off her feet. She struggled to stand even as a long rope appeared out of nowhere and tied her up from head to toe. Shrieking, Hennah flew into the air and landed far out in the ocean with a splash.

"You see something new every day!" exclaimed Norelle.

"You might, but I see the same old stuff," Rugene griped. "Except today. I liked that! Which one of us did it?"

The witches all looked at one another, but no one claimed responsibility.

Annie cleared her throat and they all turned to her. "Um, that was me, actually. Magic doesn't work on me. My mother's fairy godmother cast a spell on me for my christening gift. Magic can't touch me and it fades when I'm around."

"Really?" said Cadmilla.

Norelle stayed where she was, but the rest of the witches backed away.

"That's very interesting," Cadmilla continued when she was standing behind Norelle. "It's so interesting, in fact, that we should have heard of it before. Why do you suppose we haven't?"

"Probably because we're not from around here," said Annie. "I'm Princess Annabelle and this is my husband, Prince Liam. We just got married and we're on our grand tour. I'm from Treecrest and Liam is from Dorinocco."

"I've never heard of either place," said Cadmilla.

Rugene shook her head. "Or either of them."

"How did you get here?" asked Septicimia.

Annie glanced at Liam, not sure how to answer.

"I know how they did it," said Rugene. "They have postcards. I saw the girl put them in her pocket."

"Aagh!" shrieked a voice as something shot through the air and landed on the beach with a loud *splat!* Hennah had returned, no longer tied up with ropes. She sat up and got to her feet, spitting salt water. Reaching down the neck of her gown, she pulled out a jellyfish and tossed it back into the ocean. "That was fun!" she declared. "But I think I'll lie down for a little while." Staggering, she made her way to one of the huts and went inside.

"Let me see the postcards," said Cadmilla.

Annie was reluctant to hand them over, but she didn't see any way around it. She glanced at Liam, who shrugged and nodded. When she carried them over to Cadmilla, the witch snatched them from her hand, obviously leery of touching Annie. The witch moved away then and began to look through the cards as the other witches gathered around her.

"The top three are the only ones we haven't visited yet," Liam told them from where he stood beside Annie. "We'd like to go home now, but none of the cards would take us there."

"This one is a picture of Nastia Nautica's ship. It's right over there," Rugene said, pointing at the water. "I once made a bubble and went down there to look around. Big mistake! That sea witch is even nastier than Hennah. Nastia Nautica isn't there anymore, but I still wouldn't use a postcard to go down there unless you were a fish or could breathe underwater."

"Her ship is at the bottom of the ocean," explained Norelle. "She isn't there now because a friend of ours sent her to an ocean on the other side of the world."

"I recognize that ice castle," Septicimia said, pointing at another card. "The Blue Witch used to live there. She's moved to the enchanted forest, so she isn't there anymore. Last I heard, the abominable snowmen who used to be her servants took it over. Nasty creatures that got even nastier after she left with her magic."

"We all know this place," Cadmilla said as she turned to the last card. "That's the castle in Greater Greensward. We used to live in a retirement community there before we were tricked into coming to this island."

"If you want help getting home, that's where you should go," said Norelle. "The royal family is very nice. They helped us out when we needed it."

"Are you sure?" asked Annie. "We've heard some not-nice things about Greater Greensward."

"Don't believe a word of it," said Rugene. "They're all do-gooders, dragons included."

"Dragons?" Annie said to Liam.

"Hey," said Liam. "It sounds like the best of the three."

CHAPTER 12

ANNIE HAD TO admit, the castle in Greater Greensward was lovely. Tall towers rose above the weathered gray stones, while green banners fluttered from the spires. The drawbridge was open across the moat, where water lilies bloomed and small fish darted just below the clear water's surface. It was so much like the castle at home that a lump formed in Annie's throat and she felt truly homesick for the first time since leaving Treecrest.

"No dragons yet," Liam said, studying the sky and the land behind them.

Annie cleared her throat and said, "They probably live in caves. I'm sure I would if I were a dragon."

The postcard had brought Annie and Liam to the road at the end of the drawbridge. Although they had appeared in full view of the guards standing on either side of the portcullis, neither one reacted to their sudden arrival. When a witch flew by on a broomstick, landing inside the castle wall, neither the guards nor the people crossing the drawbridge looked up. Annie wondered if magic was so commonplace in Greater Greensward that people barely acknowledged it.

Liam took Annie's hand as they joined the people entering the castle grounds. They were partway across the drawbridge when they heard a sudden loud whooshing overhead. People cleared the courtyard, but no one panicked when two large dragons landed in front of the castle steps. One of the dragons was white tinged with blue, the other was green and more delicate looking than the first. Even from the other side of the courtyard, Annie could hear their magic. Unlike most of the other magic she had heard, this sounded like music with its own complex melody.

"Get back!" Liam shouted, shoving Annie behind him.

She stumbled on the uneven surface of the drawbridge and landed on her knees. "Ow!" she cried.

Liam had already reached for the sword on his hip when he remembered that it wasn't there. Even so, he stood between Annie and the dragons, prepared to fight. He was as startled as Annie when the light around the dragons shimmered and they both turned into humans. The green dragon was now a beautiful young woman with blond hair and vivid blue eyes, while the blue-and-white dragon had become a handsome young man with silvery white hair.

A woman passing by was helping Annie up when the two dragon people stalked toward Liam. Annie could still hear their magic, which grew louder as they approached.

"Why did you push that girl?" the young man asked Liam, sounding angry.

Liam was so surprised that he didn't seem to know what to say. "I, uh . . . what?"

"You knocked her down for no reason. Why would you do such a thing?" demanded the young woman.

Liam glanced behind him to see who they were talking about. When he saw Annie brushing off her knees, he turned back to the dragon people and said, "That isn't a girl. That's my wife. I was trying to protect her from, uh, well . . . you."

"That's true," Annie said, coming up to join him. "My husband works under the mistaken belief that I can't take care of myself."

"Really?" said the girl. "I know someone just like that." She turned and cast the silver-haired young man a look that made him shrug and give her a rueful smile.

"How did you turn from a dragon into a human?" asked Annie. "Are you both powerful witches?"

She could hear their magic more clearly now. One of them had a sweet melody with another, simpler melody running through it. The other's music was more strident and had a harsher tone. The dragon-people also had distinctive scents, although the girl's was fainter than the boy's. The girl's scent reminded Annie of burned toast, while the boy's was sour, like a piece of fruit that was starting to decay.

"Neither of us are witches," the girl said with a laugh. "My mother is a witch, though, and can turn into a dragon whenever she wants. I can, too, because she turned into one so often when she was expecting me. My husband is a dragon who had to learn how to change into a human. All dragons can do it if they learn how."

"We saw dragons like you in East Aridia," said Liam. "They were attacking the city in pairs; one exhaled gas and the other lit it with a flame."

"The dragons are at war with King Beltran. They've learned that they're much stronger when they pair an ice dragon with a fire-breather," said the girl. "I understand why they do what they do, but I could never try to hurt someone. It makes me ill just to think about it. You must be new around here. I'm Millie and this is my husband, Audun."

"Princess Millie, if you really want to know," Audun added.

"This is my wife, Princess Annabelle of Treecrest, and I'm Prince Liam of Dorinocco."

"Where are Treecrest and Dorinocco?" asked Millie. "I've never heard of either one."

"No one has lately," Annie said with a sigh. "We're far from home and want to get back, but we don't know how."

"We just got married and are on our grand tour," said Liam. "A woods witch gave us—"

"There you are!" cried a voice from the top of the stairs. A little woman with white hair waved to Millie and Audun as she hurried down the steps. "I went inside to ask where I could find you. I need your help. I have to go back to my castle to fetch something I left behind, but my eyes still aren't very good, so I can't go alone. I'd ask Mudine, but she's been having tingling in her fingers and toes, elbows and nose lately. She doesn't mind, except the tingling in her nose makes her sneeze, so she's gone off to find the witch doctor who treated her the last time she was ill. Oculura and Dyspepsia are away as well. Their cousin is getting married in Soggy Molvinia. She's holding the wedding in a swamp at midnight, so of course Oculura and Dyspepsia want to be there. Her bridesmaids are will-o'-the-wisps, and you know what they're like!"

Annie turned to Liam with a surprised look. "Dragons and will-o'-the wisps are real here! I wonder what else is real that isn't at home."

The little white-haired woman glanced at Annie and raised one eyebrow. "And who, may I ask, are you?"

"Princess Annabelle and Prince Liam, I'd like you to meet Azuria, the Blue Witch," said Audun before turning to the white-haired woman. "They aren't from around here. As far as I can tell, they aren't from any of the known kingdoms. They were telling us how they came to be here when you arrived."

"You were on your grand tour . . . ," prompted Millie.

"Oh, right! We were going to go by ship until we heard that a nasty wizard was after us. A woods witch gave us some postcards . . ." Annie glanced at Liam, who seemed surprised that she'd mentioned the cards. "We might as well show them, Liam, if we want them to help us. Anyway, she gave us the cards to use for our grand tour, then my mother's fairy god-mother said we should use them while she took care of the wizard. The only problem is, the woods witch didn't give us a card that will take us home, and the wizard has been traveling ahead of us, trying to turn people against us!"

"I guess the fairy wasn't very successful at getting rid of the wizard for you," said Audun.

"If the wizard was traveling ahead of you, he must know where you're going. Are you sure he wasn't in disguise and gave them to you himself?" asked Azuria.

"We thought of that," said Annie. "We had never met the woods witch before. But I don't think so for a number of reasons. And looking back, I didn't hear any magic when we were talking to her, and I would have if it was the wizard in disguise."

"You can hear magic?" asked the Blue Witch, looking surprised.

Annie nodded. She noticed that while Audun looked interested, Millie just smiled.

"Annie has a special talent," Liam said, sounding proud. "Magic doesn't work on her. If anyone is near her, their magic fades and goes away if they touch her. She can also hear magic, good or bad."

"I've never heard of such a thing!" cried the Blue Witch. "Imagine, magic can't touch her. I'm tempted to try a spell on her just to see what happens, but that can wait until later." She turned to Millie and Audun. "If the wizard is going ahead of them to talk to people, has he come to see you?"

"It's possible," said Millie. "Audun and I were out, and Mother and Father took my little brother, Felix, to visit my grandparents in Upper Montevista, so someone could have stopped by when no one was here."

"There's another problem," said Liam. "If we do find a way home, what's going to stop the wizard from following us there and causing even more trouble?"

"Good point," said Millie. "Maybe we can help you with that. I wouldn't want to confront him here with so many innocents around, but we could face him at Azuria's castle. There's no one there but some eagles."

"And the abominable snowmen," said Liam. "Didn't we hear that they took over the castle after the Blue Witch left?"

"They did indeed," Azuria replied. "Which is another reason I need your help. I still have a problem seeing white, and they are *snowmen*."

"We'd be happy to go with you, wouldn't we, Audun?" said Millie. "What did you forget, Azuria?"

"My map to the Magic Marketplace. I didn't notice it was missing until I wanted to go. I've run out of supplies for some potions and I need to stock up again. When I couldn't find it, I remembered that I'd left it on my bedchamber wall in the castle. Oh, dear! I just thought of something. What if the snowmen get their mittens on it and go to the marketplace? I'll be responsible for whatever havoc or mayhem they wreak. I could get my witching privileges revoked, and then where would I be? I need to get the map back as soon as possible!"

"Then we'll leave right away," said Millie. "Annie, Liam, the wizard is probably keeping track of what happens to you on each stop. If he finds out that you've gone to the castle with us, he might follow."

"But how will he know where we've gone?" asked Liam.

"I'll write a note and post it on the front door," Millie told him. "Just give me a few minutes and we can go. I need to tell the captain of the guard and then find you some warm clothes. Audun and I can carry you and Azuria. It shouldn't take more than a day to reach the Icy North."

"We could use the postcards," said Annie. "We have one for the castle and we'd get there in seconds."

"You have a postcard for my old castle!" said Azuria. "Well, I'll be! Imagine that! I've never traveled by postcard before. I wonder what they'll think of next!"

CHAPTER 13

DESPITE THE WARM clothes Millie had given them, Annie and Liam shivered as they stood in front of the ice castle. The wind coming down from the mountains dusted them with snow while reddening their cheeks and noses. Annie blew into her mittened hands as she listened to Millie and Audun debate where they should enter the castle. When Liam scooped up snow and started to make a snowball, Annie shook her head. "Don't you dare! I'm cold enough as it is without melting snow trickling down my neck."

They had arrived at the foot of the castle, which was intact as far as Annie could tell, but the others weren't so sure. "I'll look around," volunteered Audun. "We left the castle from the far side. Unless the snowmen did major repairs, it should still be in bad shape. Before we go in, I want to make sure it's not going to fall down around our ears."

Annie gasped when Audun turned into a dragon before her eyes. Although she'd seen him turn from a dragon into a human earlier that day, somehow this seemed even more amazing. She watched him beat his wings and rise into the sky. It was thrilling, especially since she'd never seen a dragon so close before.

The white dragon circled high overhead before flying back to rejoin them. When he landed, everyone crowded close to hear what he had to say. "The snowmen are working on the back of the castle. It looks as if they've already done a lot. When we left, it was nearly half-ruined, but they've fixed most of the roof and outer walls. We can try going in through the front door. We'll just have to be as quiet as possible. Sound really carries in this castle. When I was frozen in the wall, I could hear everything."

"Frozen in the wall?" Annie mouthed to Liam, who raised an eyebrow in response.

"Um, Audun, aren't you forgetting something?" Millie asked as her husband started toward the door.

"I don't think so. Were we supposed to bring something with us?"

Millie shook her head, then pointed from Audun to herself. He glanced down, only to look up and smile. "Sorry! I forgot." Light shimmered around him and once more a handsome young man with silvery white hair was standing in their midst. "The door is too small for a dragon, but fine for humans," he explained to Annie and Liam.

Everyone followed Audun to the door, which was only a few inches taller than Liam. Audun opened it without any trouble, and they all filed inside.

"I'll take it from here," whispered Azuria. "My room is back this way. Remember, be as quiet as you can."

Fascinated, Annie looked around as they tiptoed through the narrow halls. The entire castle was built of ice, most of which was blue. Although the floor was level, neither the ceiling nor the walls were straight, with strange bulges and depressions here and there. As they made their way deeper into the castle, she saw that many of the walls had been patched with white ice, which seemed to bother Azuria. The old witch muttered to herself as she walked, complaining about every change. She didn't pause until she reached her chamber, where she stopped outside the door to peer in.

"I was afraid of this," she muttered. "Two of the walls have caved in. My map is buried under chunks of ice."

"Let me look," said Audun. "Excuse me! Pardon me! Coming through!" he said, pushing his way to the front of the line. Millie was right behind him, and they slipped into the room together.

A few minutes later, Millie stuck her head out of the room. "We can handle this," she said. "I spotted some things buried in the ice. One of them might be the map. Stay out there. We need as much room as we can get."

"Don't you think we—" Azuria began, but Millie had already started to change. Soon there were two dragons in the room, making it so cramped that it was hard for them to turn around.

Annie stepped into the room to see what the dragons were doing. At first she thought they were pawing through the icy rubble, until she realized that they were digging two tunnels straight down into the ice.

"I have to say," said Azuria, "I really do appreciate that all four of you came to help me. When I lived here before, I didn't have any friends. The snowmen were here, of course, but they waited on me without ever talking. You can't imagine how lonely I felt! I'm so glad I left with Millie and her friends when I did. I live with three other witches now and I'm never lonely. One of the witches is my old childhood friend, Mudine. And I've met a man! A very nice farmer named Sam has been calling on me and I think he's about to propose. Imagine, me marrying for the first time at my age! Who would have thought? Say, what's that little blue thing?"

Millie and Audun had started tossing things out of the tunnels. One of them was a small blue object made of yarn. Azuria scurried to pick it up, exclaiming, "It's my nose warmer! I haven't seen that in ages! At last I'll have a warm nose again."

Annie giggled when the old woman slipped two loops around her ears and pulled a cone made of knit yarn over her nose. The tassel at the tip of her nose bobbed each time she spoke. "This is so handy when I go outside. A friend made it for me years ago."

A tiny bottle flew out of a tunnel, landing on the ice with a *thunk!* Azuria picked it up, squealing with delight. "It's my special secret potion for upset tummies! Oh, and here's my favorite nightcap with the earflaps. My head will be so much warmer tonight!"

Annie laughed as the witch hurried around, picking up the objects as they flew out of the tunnel. When something creaked farther down the hallway, Liam tapped Annie's arm and put his finger to his lips. Turning to listen, she could hear the faint slap of feet and scrape of claws. She glanced at Azuria, who was chortling over her finds, but the witch was looking the other way and there was no way to get her attention without calling out to her.

Liam was standing in front of Annie when two snowmen stomped around a bulge in the hallway. She had half expected them to look like the yetis, but although they were as large and covered with white fur, their faces were very different. Where the yetis' faces looked almost human under their fur, the snowmen's furry faces looked more like animals. Their small, red-rimmed eyes held a nasty gleam when they spotted

Liam and Annie, and when they opened their mouths, their long teeth looked sharper than wolves' fangs.

"Uh, Azuria, we have company," Annie said over her shoulder.

The witch trotted to the doorway, her arms loaded down with miscellaneous belongings. "Is it the snowmen?" she asked. When the snowmen spotted her, the one in the front growled deep in his throat.

Dropping her belongings, Azuria pointed a finger at the furry white creatures. A wall of ice formed only a few feet in front of them, blocking the hallway and making them appear wavy and distorted. The wall looked as if it was thicker in some spots and thinner in others. "Drat!" said Azuria. "That wasn't what I meant to do."

"It's probably because I'm here," said Annie. "I might be making your magic weaker."

With a roar, both snowmen charged, slamming into the wall of ice with their shoulders. The entire wall shook, and cracks appeared where the ice was thinnest.

The snowmen roared and pounded on the wall, while Azuria bent down to retrieve the items she had dropped. "That wall won't hold for long," she told Annie and Liam. "We need to get out of here."

Millie popped out of the tunnel holding a crumpled tapestry between two of her talons. "Found it!" she exclaimed. "What's the commotion about? I could hear you all the way . . . oh!"

When Audun shot out of his tunnel, he was scowling and poison gas was leaking from his nostrils. "I'd recognize those voices anywhere. Millie, get ready. I'll blow poison gas at them and you—"

Annie had been watching the snowmen through the ice and saw when they spotted the dragons. Their arms dropped to their sides and their mouths snapped shut. A moment later they were gone, having run back the way they had come.

Azuria chuckled and grinned from ear to ear. "They remember you, all right! The last thing they want to do is tangle with you two again. I bet some of them are still singed around the edges from your last meeting."

"Do you think they'll leave us alone now that they know the dragons are here?" asked Annie.

"I'm sure of it," Azuria replied. "They probably won't be back until they're certain we're long gone."

Liam glanced from Azuria to the dragons. "So what do we do now? Do you still want to wait around for Rotan to show up?"

"I think we should," said Audun. "Even a wizard couldn't do much harm here."

Azuria yawned and patted her mouth with her hand. "I don't know about you young people, but all this excitement has worn me out. I think we should look around and see if there are any rooms fit to sleep in. It will be dark here soon, and we should settle down for the night before then."

"Would it be possible to have a fire in one of the fireplaces?" asked Annie. "Just enough to take off the chill?"

Azuria shook her head. "The fireplaces are for decoration only. They're made of ice, just like the walls. You light a fire in one of them and the ice would melt. Then we'd have a real mess! But if you're cold, we'll look for blankets. They might be a little musty, but they should still get you warm!"

With the dragons leading the way, they explored the castle, skirting the rubble that half filled some of the hallways, trying doors that were blocked on the other side and stepping over cracks that ran from one wall to another. They found a few rooms with intact walls and floors, but the ceilings looked questionable and they didn't dare set foot inside. The kitchen had been destroyed, as had the great hall and two other rooms nearby. In one room, the ceiling had caved in completely.

"This is the chamber I shared with my friend Zoë," said Millie. "It's where I first realized that Audun's family was frozen in the walls."

"That's horrible!" said Annie.

"The snowmen did it," Millie explained. "They didn't like company who might take Azuria away, so they tried to scare people off. Until my friends and I came, the dragons were the only ones who made it this far. The snowmen froze them in the castle walls before Azuria knew they were here."

"The snowmen thought they could steal my object of power and keep it for themselves," said Azuria. "Not one of them came close to guessing that it was my old shoe!"

"How about this room?" Audun called from farther down the hall. "It looks safe enough and there are three beds. That's all we need. Millie and I don't need beds when we're dragons."

"I think this is where my cousin Francis and the troll Simon-Leo slept," said Millie.

"This will do just fine," Azuria assured them. "See, there are already blankets on the bed. Now, who's hungry? I haven't lost my knack for using my magic to make food, so we can eat whatever you want."

"I had a taste of chocolate once. Do you think you could make that?" asked Liam.

"Sure," Azuria told him. "Any other requests?"

"Will your magic work while I'm around?" asked Annie.

Azuria tapped her chin with one finger. "Hmm, good point! Go stand down the hall and I'll call you when it's ready. I use magic to make the food, but once it's made, it's regular food, so you shouldn't have any problem eating it!"

Annie stepped down the hall far enough that she couldn't hear her friends talking. When they finally called to her, she hurried back to see a tablecloth spread across one of the beds and the surface covered with tempting dishes. They had a feast of everyone's favorite foods then, which meant Annie ate a lot of pastries. She was trying to decide if she could manage to eat one more tart when Azuria declared that it was time for bed. "Don't worry!" she told them. "I'll make a nice breakfast in the morning!"

"How do we wash the dishes?" Annie asked as she got to her feet.

"We won't," Azuria told her. "My magic will do it for us."

With a flourish of her hand, a plate of pickles disappeared and one or two other dishes shivered but didn't actually go anywhere. "Uh, would you mind leaving the room again?" she asked Annie.

Annie strode back down the hall. When she returned, the bed was cleared off and there wasn't a scrap of food in sight. Azuria was climbing into bed wearing a nightgown, her nose warmer, and the nightcap with earflaps.

"I put an extra blanket on that bed for you," Liam told Annie, pointing at the bed beside the Blue Witch's. "I'll sleep in this other one, and Millie and Audun are going to sleep just outside the door in case the snowmen come back."

"Good!" said Annie, wondering if she should warn the others that Liam snored.

౭ఎ

When Annie woke the next morning, Azuria's bed was empty and Liam was pulling on his heavy winter coat.

Seeing Annie roll over, he said, "Time to get up. Azuria went down the hall to look at something she called a far-seeing ball. She said she couldn't see anything in it when she was in the room with you."

Annie got out of bed and pulled her outer coat off the blankets where she'd draped it for extra warmth. "What does this far-seeing ball do?" she asked as she stuck her arm into a coat sleeve.

"It helps you see things far away," Azuria said as she came back into the room. "Or close up, like that wizard you're so worried about. He's lurking outside the castle, waiting for us to come out."

"Now what?" Annie asked Millie. "We never did talk about what we'd do when we saw him."

"Now we capture him and take him somewhere he can't hurt anyone ever again," said Audun. "And I know just where that will be."

"I have a feeling that catching him is going to be the hard part," Liam told him. "Rotan isn't going to sit still so we can tie him up."

"I have my ways," said Azuria. "Let's go do this while I'm still feeling fresh."

Audun led the way out the front door. Azuria came next, ready with a spell to repel any attack of Rotan's. Liam followed her armed with a sword that the witch had conjured for him. Annie came next so she could hold on to Liam and protect him from the wizard's magic. She was also in charge of the cloth sack Azuria had found to carry the belongings she'd retrieved. Millie was the last out the door, and was so warm from keeping her internal fire stoked and ready for flaming that ice melted underfoot with each step she took.

They didn't see Rotan when they walked outside, but they had gone only a short distance from the castle before he hailed them from the top of a nearby hill.

"So you made it this far!" he shouted at Annie and Liam. "I'm surprised. I never thought you could do it. Most royals would be too weak and timid to get past the first few postcards. It's a shame you didn't visit Nastia Nautica's ship. That would have taken care of you once and for all! You were either braver, smarter, or luckier than I thought possible. Ah, well, I can't have you going home to mess up my plans, so now it's up to me. Get away from there, old woman. I don't have any quarrels with you. And take your lizards with you. Their kind has no place in this."

"Our kind?" Millie growled. "What does he mean by that?"

"We don't have dragons like you where we come from," Annie told her. "Unless he was in East Aridia when the dragons attacked, he's probably never seen one before. I bet he has no idea what you and Audun are capable of doing. He probably thinks you're animals and not very smart."

Tiny flames licked Millie's lips when she said, "Then maybe we can surprise him."

"Not yet," said Azuria. "Save the surprise in case we need it later. Let's see if I can handle this."

Holding her head high, the little witch walked forward twenty paces so she was closer to the wizard and far enough from Annie that her magic would work. "You've made this my fight by following us here!" she shouted. "This is between you and me now!" Azuria was flexing her wrists, preparing to cast a spell, when Rotan raised a slender wand above his head, a look of confidence on his face. Sparks flared at the end of the wand when he lowered it and pointed it at Annie and Liam, ignoring Azuria altogether. Annie's hand shot out and grabbed Liam's shoulder. When the magic from the wand hit them, it bounced back and enveloped the wizard in an orange light. He staggered, trying to keep his balance.

Azuria turned to talk to her friends. "He uses a wand! Only minor wizards use wands to focus their power. Strong wizards don't need them!"

"Watch out!" Annie told her as Rotan raised his wand again.

"I did that on purpose!" the wizard shouted. "I wanted to see if magic really can't touch you, Princess. Now I know what I have to do."

"The old blowhard can't stop talking, can he?" said Azuria. "Let's show him that actions really do speak louder than words!" Pointing her finger at the snowdrift at the base of the castle, she muttered something under her breath. Annie gasped as snow collected, forming a ball twenty feet across. With a twitch of Azuria's finger, the ball shot toward the hill where the wizard was waving his wand in the air. Seconds before the snowball hit him, a terrific gust of wind blew it aside.

"Huh!" said Azuria. "I guess he didn't get my point. Maybe this will get it across." This time when she pointed at the castle, an icicle as long as her arm broke off the roof and hurtled toward Rotan. The wizard's gust of wind was too weak to stop the ice spear, and he had to throw himself into the snow to avoid it. When he got back on his feet, he no longer looked quite so confident.

"Is it my turn yet?" asked Millie.

"Not yet," said Azuria. "I think it's time I try something a little stronger." The witch had just raised her hand when Rotan crawled to the top of the hill on his knees and aimed his wand at the sky. Snow began to fall so thick and fast that it was soon impossible to see.

"Oh, no you don't!" said Azuria. With her finger pointed at the ground, she stomped her foot three times. A crack opened in the ice, running straight to where they had last seen the wizard. Even while the crack was spreading, Azuria waved her finger again. A wind sprang up, blowing the falling snow at the hillside in a miniature blizzard. When the snow cleared, the wizard was no longer there.

Annie couldn't tell if Azuria had blown the wizard off the hill or if he had fallen into the crack in the ice. She was waiting for him to reappear when a heart-stopping roar shook the ground. A sea of white flowed over and around the hill like a churning spring flood. The snowmen were back, in force this time, and they were charging straight at the group of friends.

"I thought you said they wouldn't come back until they were sure we were gone," shouted Liam.

"He must have placed a compulsion on them," Azuria cried as she created walls of ice to block the snowmen. Each time a wall appeared in front of them, they beat at it until they had broken through, even after their hands were cut and bloody. "It's a powerful compulsion, too. They won't stop until it wears off or they die."

"I don't want to hurt them if someone is making them do this!" said Annie. "Isn't there anything we can do?"

"Get on Millie's back," Audun told her. "You, too, Liam. Azuria, you're riding with me. It's time we take this fight to my stomping ground. He's involving innocents here, but there are no innocents where we're going."

"And where is that?" asked Liam as he helped Annie onto the dragon's back.

"The ice-dragon stronghold," said Audun. "Millie, we're going to have to pace ourselves so that he won't be able to catch up, but we won't lose him. We want him to follow us all the way there so we can end this once and for all!"

Chapter 14

RIDING ON THE back of a dragon had to be the most exhilarating thing Annie had ever done. She was perched on Millie's back with her arms wrapped around Liam, grinning as her hair whipped behind her and the wind brought tears to her eyes.

"I never thought dragons were real, and now we're riding one!" she shouted into Liam's ear.

"Look at those mountains!" he shouted back. "Can you believe we're flying above them?"

"I can't believe any of this! We must be dreaming!"

They were straddling the base of Millie's neck, well in front of her powerful wings. When Annie closed her eyes, she could almost imagine she was riding a horse bareback; Millie's neck was about the same diameter as a horse's barrel and the movement of her muscles created a rocking sort of motion. Annie liked it best when Millie stilled her wings to glide, letting the air currents carry her. Without the *whump! whump!* of her beating wings, the only sound was that of the air rushing past. Their flight was so smooth that it almost felt as if they weren't moving at all.

As excited as she was, Annie almost forgot that they had a reason to ride on a dragon's back. Every once in a while she remembered and turned around to look behind them. Rotan was there, sitting astride a crooked branch that still bore a few withered, ice-coated leaves. He flew hunched over with both hands gripping the branch, so intent on following the dragons that he didn't seem to notice the wind that made his long robes flap behind him. Annie thought he looked like a predatory bird, ready to strike. Just looking at him was enough to make her shiver.

Annie was glad that she and Liam were riding on Millie's back and not Audun's. Millie was keeping her internal fire stoked so that her body generated enough heat to keep her passengers warm. Annie felt toasty from her head to her toes despite the cold weather. As an ice dragon, Audun couldn't generate heat, and actually felt cold to the touch. Riding on him would only have made Annie colder, whereas Azuria had magic to make warmer clothes for herself.

Although the air was bitterly cold when they started out, it became even colder as they headed over the mountains and Annie could finally see the ocean. Unlike the clear blue water surrounding the islands they had visited in warmer climates, the water here was a murky blue gray that hid whatever was in its depths. When Annie looked straight ahead, she could see a cloud bank that stretched from one side of the horizon to the other. The clouds were thick and dark, piling on top of each other so high that she wondered if any dragon could fly over them.

Annie glanced down and gasped. A group of large fish were racing through the water below them. One came to the surface and blew water out of a hole on top of its head. Another rose up, then fell back into the water with a tremendous splash.

"Those are whales," Millie called, turning her head toward Annie and Liam. "They look big from here, but they're enormous when you get close. The smaller one is a baby."

"Amazing!" Annie exclaimed.

She was still watching the whales when something screamed. When she looked up, she saw a flock of large birds tearing toward them out of the sky. Half the birds peeled off to attack Audun, while the rest came after Millie. Some of the birds flew at the dragoness, pecking at her head and face. The others descended on Annie and Liam.

"Get down, Annie!" Liam shouted as he waved the sword Azuria had given to him.

Annie crouched behind him, but when she felt a bird's talons on her back, she turned and flung up her arm. The bird was about to tear at her when she struck it, and suddenly it seemed more anxious to get away than attack her. She turned to look; the bird that had appeared to be some kind of large hawk was now a seagull. It flew away, squawking in distress.

"They're not hawks, they're seagulls!" Annie shouted. "Rotan changed them!"

"If he wants hawks, he can have them!" cried Azuria, waving her finger in the air.

A strong wind sprang up to blow the birds back to the wizard. He flailed his arms at them so violently that he nearly fell off his branch. Annie watched him until she had to hold on more tightly to Liam; Millie was descending toward the water.

The two dragons were flying side by side under the clouds now. A cold wind lashed them with sleet, which froze on Audun but dripped off the warmer Millie. When water ran into Annie's eyes, she let go of Liam long enough to wipe her face with the back of her hand. Dropping her hand, she happened to glance down and gasped as a black-and-white fish as long as Millie shot out of the water straight at them, its teeth-lined jaws gaping open.

"Watch out!" Annie screamed.

Millie's head whipped down. "Hang on!" she shouted, veering to the side. With a few powerful beats of her wings, they were angled higher again, entering the thick gray clouds.

They flew through the clouds for a time, unable to see anything around them. Even so, Millie and Audun stayed close together, apparently able to know exactly where the other dragon was in the murky darkness.

"How can you fly through this without getting lost?" Annie called to Millie after they'd been in the clouds for a while.

"Dragons have an excellent sense of direction," Millie called back. "We can find any place even with our eyes closed as long as we've been there before."

"Are we almost there?" asked Annie.

Millie chuckled, which made her shake so hard that Annie could feel the vibration under her. "We're still a few hours away," the dragoness finally said.

When the clouds around them finally parted, revealing a dismal sky and the leaden-looking ocean below, Annie felt as if a weight had been lifted off her. She glanced at Audun, who was flying so close to Millie that the two dragons' wing tips almost touched. Azuria had used her magic to wrap herself in a layer of blankets and was tied onto the dragon with straps. She was asleep, her head lolling with each beat of Audun's wings, her mittened hands lying limply at her sides. Every once in a while she jerked awake, consulted her far-seeing ball, and said something to Audun. Within minutes, her eyes were closed again. Apparently she didn't find dragon flight as exciting as Annie and Liam did.

Annie glanced back, wondering if they had lost Rotan. When she didn't see him, she called to Millie, "I think we've lost the wizard."

"He's still there," said Millie. "He's just farther behind. Azuria is keeping track of him with her far-seeing ball."

Millie was right. The next time Annie looked back, Rotan was in sight, clutching the branch, looking more bedraggled than ever.

It wasn't long before Annie started seeing huge blocks of ice floating in the water. "What are those?" she asked Liam. When he didn't know, she asked Millie.

"Those are called icebergs. This part of the ocean is full of them. Now that we've seen them, we know that we're a little over an hour away from the stronghold."

"That's good," said Annie, "because—" She gasped as a wall of water rose out of the ocean to tower over their heads.

"Rotan!" exclaimed Liam.

"Oh, no he doesn't!" Millie cried as the wall began to descend on them.

Annie could feel the dragoness take in a deep breath and was amazed when she exhaled a long tongue of flame that grew bigger with each passing second. The water wall shrank as the flame turned it into steam, which Azuria blew back at Rotan. Annie looked behind her when the wizard yelped and nearly fell off his branch again.

They flew in and out of clouds after that. Millie's heat was enough to warm Annie and Liam and to dry their clothes once they were out in the open. The next time the dragons began to descend, they headed toward the largest iceberg Annie had seen yet. It was higher than the tallest icebergs they had passed and wider than most, with sides as sheer as if a giant had used a knife to cut them from an even bigger block of ice. When the clouds opened up above them, letting the sun shine through, the whole thing reflected light like a polished mirror.

The reflected light was so bright that Annie didn't notice the three approaching dragons at first. It didn't help that they were as white as the iceberg and blended in so well with it. Audun and Millie saw them right away, however, and flew to meet them.

"We need your help, Wave Diver. An evil wizard is following us!" Audun shouted to the leader of the dragons. "Tell Frostybreath!"

"We can do the same thing to this wizard that we did to Olebald!" Wave Diver shouted back.

"That's what I was thinking!" Audun replied.

While Wave Diver landed on the ice and disappeared into an almost invisible opening, the other two dragon guards moved off so that they blended in with the ice again, making it almost impossible for Rotan to see them. Millie landed at the entrance right behind Wave Diver and slipped into a tunnel that could easily fit two dragons side by side. Annie crinkled her nose. The air smelled sour, almost as if bushels of fruit had gone bad. It took her a moment to recognize it as the concentrated smell of many ice dragons living together.

"Go wait at the end of the hall," Wave Diver told Millie. "Audun knows what to do. He'll lure the wizard in, then my dragons will follow and block the entrance so the wizard can't escape that way."

Liam was already helping Annie down from Millie's back when he turned to Wave Diver and asked, "Is there anything I can do to help?"

The dragon, who was nearly twice as long as Millie, just laughed. "Not a thing, little human, except stay out of the way. We can handle this. Now hurry. I can hear a human shouting. The wizard must be close."

Annie and Liam ran down the hall with Millie right behind. Although everything was made of ice, the floor had been embedded with sand so that it wasn't slippery. The hall was fiercely cold, however, and Annie already regretted that she and Liam had been so quick to get off Millie's back. Annie's teeth were chattering when they reached the end of the hall.

"You two wait inside," said Millie, and nudged them toward an open door. They slipped inside, but instead of hiding, they peered around the doorway.

Another dragon joined Millie. He wasn't much bigger than she was and had an officious air about him.

"Wave Diver sent for Frostybreath. What is going on? I should be kept informed at all times so I can inform the king."

"Hello, Iceworthy," said Millie. "It's an evil wizard named Rotan. He's followed us here and we want Frostybreath to freeze him. The wizard should be entering the hall at any moment."

"Oh!" said the dragon, and he scurried off around the corner.

"You should go back inside," Millie told Annie and Liam, shuffling closer as if to block the doorway.

Annie glanced down. Millie was so warm that the floor under her feet was partially melted. When she moved, the floor refroze instantly, almost as if by magic.

"Is there magic here?" Annie asked her. "Does magic keep the stronghold together? Because if it does, my presence here will bring it down around us. Remember, we told you that magic doesn't work around me."

"Don't worry," said Millie. "Your being here won't make a bit of difference. The stronghold is held together through dragon magic, which is the strongest magic of all. Nothing can hurt this place."

The thunder of running dragon feet came from around the corner. "I hope that's Frostybreath," Millie said, and turned her head to see who was there. A moment later Audun landed in the entrance and Azuria hopped off, calling, "Rotan is right behind us!"

The Blue Witch hurried down the hall and threw herself into the room. After taking one look at Annie, who was turning blue, Azuria asked, "Are you cold?" When Annie nodded, the witch pointed a finger and sent blue sparkles her way. The sparkles hit Annie and rebounded, splatting across Azuria's chest, then growing to envelop her. A moment later the old witch was wearing another layer of thick, fuzzy clothes. "Drat! I forgot about you and magic! Here, I don't need these, you do." Taking off the extra clothes, she handed them to Annie and glanced at Liam.

"I'm fine," he said.

Annie gave Azuria a grateful smile as she drew the warmer clothes over the ones she was wearing. She was pulling up the hood when Rotan shot into the hall and hopped off his branch. Suddenly Audun was running down the corridor toward them. "Run, Millie!" he shouted as Azuria dragged Annie and Liam away from the door.

A hissing sound followed Liam down the hall. He was halfway to the corner when the ceiling above his head cracked in long, jagged lines. An instant later it was whole again and looked as if it had never been touched.

Rotan swore and tried again, aiming at the floor. The new crack repaired itself just as quickly.

Audun had almost reached the corner when Rotan said a spell over his walking stick, turning it into a spear and hurling it at Liam. "It's poisoned!" Azuria shouted.

Millie's head popped around the corner. She flamed, aiming it at the stick, which blackened and turned into ash.

As the wizard drew closer, Annie could hear his next spell forming. Whatever it was, the noise it made was harsh and discordant. "We have to stop him!" Annie told Liam.

He nodded. Waiting until Rotan was passing the open doorway, Liam dashed out of the room and tackled the wizard, knocking him to the floor. Annie was right behind him, and before Rotan could catch his breath, she had her hand on his arm. The moment she touched him, his magic fizzled and went out.

"What did you do?" Rotan shouted just as a huge white-and-blue dragon came tearing around the corner.

Annie and Liam got out of the way as the dragon took a deep breath and blew a coating of frost on Rotan. Ice crackled as it formed on the wizard, holding him immobile so that only his eyes could move.

"Thank you, Frostybreath," said Audun. "He was a hard one to stop."

"He doesn't look like much," the big dragon said, giving the wizard a poke with his talon. "How evil is he?"

"As bad as Olebald," said Millie. "And he deserves to be put on ice for a good long time."

"Then that is precisely what we'll do," Frostybreath said as he picked up the motionless wizard with his talons and draped him over one shoulder.

Six other dragons came racing around the corner, skidding to a stop when they saw Frostybreath with the wizard. "You got him!" one of the dragons said, sounding disappointed.

"At least we get to see what happens next!" another dragon said with glee.

They hurried to form a line behind Frostybreath, who led them around the corner to a curving ramp that ran down into the stronghold.

"This is the fastest way down," said Audun. "It's meant for dragons, so you should go with us."

After the other dragons took their turns sliding down the ramp, Millie led Annie and Liam to the starting point. Crouching down with her chin nearly touching the floor, the dragoness placed Annie on one side of her snout and Liam on the other. With her talons curled around them to hold them in place, she pushed off and started to slide.

Annie held on to Millie's arm, keeping her eyes closed at first, but when she heard Liam's delighted shout, her eyes flew open and she hazarded a look around. A moment later she was laughing with joy. The floor of the ramp was smooth without a bump or blemish to mar the ride, and they slid, twisting and turning as the tunnel changed direction. Annie felt as if she were flying again, only this time no dragon muscles bunched beneath her and there was no wind to buffet her.

The tunnel wound around and around the stronghold where the translucent walls changed from light to dark as clouds passed overhead. When it suddenly grew dark and stayed that way, Annie decided that they must have gone below the water level. And then they were sliding on polished stone, heading into the island that was the base of the stronghold.

Suddenly they were shooting off the bottom of the darkened ramp onto a floor that wasn't quite as smooth; it was enough to slow them down so they could get their feet under them and stand. Torches flickered on the walls, giving them enough light to see where they were going. They had scarcely gotten out of the way when Audun and Azuria slid off the ramp behind them. Annie's heart was still racing as they caught up with the other dragons, joining the procession that wound through the hallways to a locked door. When Annie peered around the dragons in front of her, she could see Frostybreath talking to a dragon standing guard. After a conversation that she couldn't hear, the guard unlocked the door and stepped aside. The dragons filed into the room with Frostybreath in the lead.

It was a long, narrow room with no other door. The guard had given a lit torch to one of the dragons behind Frostybreath. Without it, the room would have been completely dark, so Annie was surprised to see a motionless figure standing against one of the walls. When the dragon holding the torch moved closer, Annie could see that the figure was a bald-headed man encased in ice. His eyes were closed and he appeared to be asleep.

"This looks like a good spot," Frostybreath said, dumping Rotan on the floor. When the wizard stirred, trying to raise his hand, the big dragon breathed on him again, coating him with so much frost that he was completely white and couldn't possibly move. His eyes were closed now, and he, too, looked as if he was asleep.

Two other dragons helped Frostybreath prop Rotan against the wall beside the first figure. With his friends holding the wizard in place, Frostybreath took an extra-big breath and exhaled long and hard all over the wizard. As his friends moved out of the way, he took another breath and another, breathing on Rotan until the man was encased in a block of ice.

"There!" said Frostybreath as he admired what he had done. "Now he won't be bothering anyone."

"Is he dead?" Annie asked Millie.

The dragoness shook her head. "Not at all. When he thaws, he'll be just like he was before he was frozen even if he stays this way for hundreds of years. It's another of Frostybreath's talents."

"Apparently there's a lot more we don't know about dragons than we realized," said Liam.

"I'm constantly learning new things about dragons myself," said Millie. "And I am one!"

CHAPTER 15

ANNIE WAS RELIEVED to walk out of the room, knowing that the dragons would keep Rotan frozen for many years to come. Now that the wizard could no longer cause trouble, she and Liam could go home—if only they could find a way.

She was wondering if Millie and Audun had any idea how to help them get home, when Iceworthy stopped them in the hall. "King Stormclaw requests your presence in his audience chamber," the dragon said with his snout in the air. "You, too, Audun and Millie." He turned and walked away so quickly that Annie and Liam had to run to catch up. Azuria was muttering to herself as she scurried after them.

They followed Iceworthy to a stairwell and started to climb. The steps were wide and deep enough for dragon feet, so were bigger than normal stairs. By the time Annie got used to the rhythm of climbing them, they had gone up two levels and Iceworthy was waiting for them by another doorway.

"Wait inside the first room," he told them. "Someone will take you into the audience chamber when King Stormclaw is ready."

Annie, Liam, and Azuria went in first. It seemed like a large room until Millie and Audun joined them and nearly filled up all the space. "Why does the king want to see us?" Annie asked the two dragons. "Have we done something wrong by bringing Rotan here?"

Audun shook his head. "I don't think so," he said, although he didn't look too sure.

"Maybe we broke a rule or something," said Annie.

"If we did, it was one we don't know," Liam told her. "Let's just wait and see. Maybe it isn't anything bad."

Annie was imagining all sorts of dire punishments for those who anger the dragon king until she saw that Liam was inspecting the room. "Have you noticed that there are no seams or gaps between the walls and the floors?" he asked when he saw her looking his way. "This place is amazing!"

"Dragon magic, remember?" said Annie.

The door into the next room opened and an elderly dragon peered in at them. "King Stormclaw is ready for you now," he said. "Audun, hello, my boy! And Millie, you're here as well! It's so good to see you both!"

"Hello, Grandfather," said Audun. "What are you doing here?"

"Your grandmother lives here now, so I decided to join her. I'm teaching the young ones and fill in where I'm needed, and—" The old dragon glanced behind him as if someone else was talking. "What? Oh, yes, I'm getting them. We'll be right there!" When he turned back, he winked at his grandson. "Some dragons are very impatient. You and I can talk later. We mustn't keep the king waiting!"

The old dragon shuffled backward into the next room, leaving the door open. Millie and Audun followed him while Annie glanced at Liam. "He didn't seem angry. Maybe the king isn't, either."

"If it gets bad, we can always use a postcard and leave," Liam said, patting his pocket.

"I hope it doesn't come to that," Annie murmured as they left the room.

Taking Liam's hand, Annie stepped into the audience chamber and stopped. Azuria bumped into her and was about to complain, when she looked up and saw the room. Far larger than any great hall Annie had ever seen, the room was imposing, with its high ice ceiling and polished black stone floor that reflected the light coming through the walls of ice. It occurred to Annie that this was where the ice levels ended and the stone levels began, making an impressive setting for the audience chamber.

Aside from Annie and her friends, the end of the room where they stood was empty. At the opposite end of the audience chamber, five stone pillars supported life-size dragon statues. Annie and her friends were crossing the smooth stone floor when one of the statues moved and Annie realized that they were real, living dragons. She could hear their magic now; somehow the different melodies seemed to blend together, although one was more distinctive than the others.

Even from a distance the one in the middle looked huge; up close he would be enormous. "That has to be King Stormclaw," murmured Annie.

Audun led the way. When he was still a good distance from the pillars, he stopped and bowed his head. Millie hurried to stand beside him and do the same.

"I think you're supposed to bow," Annie whispered to Liam as they joined their friends. Liam nodded and when he bowed, Annie curtsied, which wasn't easy in the heavy layers of clothes she was wearing. Azuria made a half curtsy while mumbling about her aching back.

"At least they have manners," the dragoness with the gray-tinged scales grumbled. "I don't mean your grandson and his wife, Song! We know that they're polite! I mean the humans. Most of them are so uncivilized."

"That's quite all right, Frostweaver. I agree with you completely," said the stately dragoness seated beside the king.

"Ahem!" When the king cleared his throat, both dragonesses grew silent. "Welcome, Millie! Welcome,

Audun!" said the king in a deep voice that carried throughout the room. "It is good to see you again. I've been told that you brought us another evil wizard to keep on ice."

"Yes, Your Majesty," said Audun. "His name is Rotan. He has been stirring up trouble throughout the human kingdoms. Rotan was plaguing our friends Princess Annabelle and Prince Liam when they came to us for help. Our friend Azuria, the Blue Witch, fought him with great skill, but still he would not be vanquished. We came to you in hope that you would stop his rampage, which Frostybreath did this very day."

"I do so like it when dragons talk in the formal style like that," said the dragoness seated on the other side of Audun's grandmother. "Everyone did it when I was a girl."

"I apologize if bringing the wizard here was an imposition, Your Majesty, but it was the only place I could think of where someone would know what to do," Audun told them.

The king waved his forepaw, dismissing Audun's apology. "I quite understand," he declared. "No one can handle such matters as well as ice dragons. You were right in bringing him here. Tell me, are these three humans the people you mentioned?"

"They are," Audun told him. "King Stormclaw, may I introduce Princess Annabelle of Treecrest and Prince Liam of Dorinocco. And this is Azuria, the

Blue Witch, who now resides in the enchanted forest in Greater Greensward. You remember her, don't you, Grandmother?"

"Of course I do," said the dragoness. "We met during that horrible incident with the snowmen. Hello, Azuria! I hope you have recovered from your ordeal."

"I'm just fine now," said Azuria. "Thanks for asking!"

"Why did you not turn to Millie's mother, the Green Witch?" the king asked Audun.

"Because she was in Upper Montevista visiting my grandparents King Bodamin and Queen Frazzela," said Millie.

"I haven't seen Frazzie in ages," said Song of the Glacier. "How is she doing?"

"Quite well," Millie replied. "The last time I saw her, she spoke of inviting you to visit her again."

"I'd like that!" said Song of the Glacier. "We had so much fun the last time I visited Upper Montevista. I took her on a tour of her mountains. She loved seeing them from the air! And she served the most marvelous eels every night I was there!"

"If we have finished hearing about your visit, may I proceed?" grumbled the king.

"Of course!" said Song of the Glacier, but Annie noticed that she gave Millie a warm smile.

"You say your friends are from Treecrest and Dorinocco," said the king. "I've never heard these names before. Are they south of Aridia?"

"I don't know where they are, Your Majesty, except I don't believe they're anywhere near the kingdoms we've heard about," said Audun. "Our friends used magic postcards to get here and aren't sure which direction they'd have to head to go home."

"How interesting! Do you have these postcards with you?" the king asked, speaking to Annie and Liam for the first time.

Annie gave Liam a glance and nodded. "I have them right here, Your Majesty," said Liam as he reached into his pocket. When he pulled out the postcards, he held them up so the king could see them.

"Bring them to me, Audun," the king said, leaning down and squinting. "They are quite small and I would like to inspect them for myself."

Liam seemed reluctant to hand the postcards over, but there was no way around it. He glanced at Annie and shrugged before giving them to Audun. Annie squeezed Liam's hand. She could understand his reluctance; the cards had rescued them more than once. However, the dragons seemed honorable and she doubted they would try to keep the postcards.

The king seemed to find the cards fascinating. He examined each one before turning to Liam and saying, "How do they work?

"Just put your finger on the picture and wish you were there," said Audun.

King Stormclaw hurriedly gave the cards back to Audun. "They are most definitely not for me," he said.

"Put your finger on the picture ... That sounds like the way you get to the Magic Marketplace," said Song of the Glacier as Audun returned the cards to Liam.

"Where did you get the postcards?" asked the king.

"A witch gave them to us as a wedding gift," said Annie. "Liam and I just got married."

"I bet the witch bought them at the Magic Marketplace," Azuria announced. "I haven't been there in a long time, so I don't know what new things they might have, but the postcards sound like something they would sell there."

"Do you think they'd have postcards for Treecrest or Dorinocco?" Annie asked, feeling hopeful for the first time in days. If they could get postcards for either kingdom, they could return home that very night.

Azuria shrugged. "Probably."

"My mother has a tapestry that's a map for the marketplace on the wall of her tower. We could go back to Greater Greensward and use it," said Millie.

"That isn't necessary," declared Song of the Glacier. "I have a map for the marketplace in my chamber. You may use it if you'd like."

"Have you forgotten already?" Azuria asked Annie and Liam. "We went to my castle to find my old map. I have it right here!" She reached into the sack that held the possessions she had retrieved from the ruins of her chamber and pulled out a torn scrap of parchment.

"It looks awfully dirty," said Millie.

"And quite small," agreed Song of the Glacier. "I suggest you use mine. It's much larger and you can all place your fingers on the wall surrounding the fountain at once."

"You touch the picture of the wall surrounding the fountain if you want to go to the marketplace," Azuria explained to the king.

"Will you be leaving soon?" asked King Stormclaw.

"We'd very much like to, if you don't mind, Your Majesty," said Liam. "Annie and I are both anxious to get home. If there's a chance they sell the postcards we need at the marketplace, we'd like to go there as soon as possible."

"I understand," the king replied. "Song, why don't you take these young humans to your chamber and show them your map? Audun, I expect you to go with them and help them find this postcard vendor, then report back to me. I'd like to hear more about this marketplace and what they sell."

"I'm going, too!" said Millie. "I haven't been there since the last time my mother took me, and that was before Felix was born."

"I was going anyway," Azuria declared. "I even have my shopping list with me."

King Stormclaw was climbing down from his pillar when Audun's grandfather came over. "I'll see you when you come back," he told Audun. "I could use a visit with some friendly faces. I can't tell if your grandmother is happy I'm here or not, and the king has made it plain that he doesn't like me."

"Millie and I shouldn't be gone long," Audun promised. "We can have dinner together tonight."

"I look forward to it," his grandfather said, looking pleased.

CHAPTER 16

ANNIE WAS UNCOMFORTABLE from the moment she stepped into Song of the Glacier's suite. Everything was oversize to fit a dragon. There was polished wood furniture everywhere, from a table long enough to seat a dozen full-size dragons, to cupboards with carved-front drawers depicting dragons, and oddly shaped seats where a dragon might rest. Most of the seats were cushioned with rich, patterned fabric. Annie might have thought they looked inviting if she had been twice her size. As it was, the room and the furniture in it made her feel tiny and insignificant, a feeling she really didn't like.

Annie was still looking around when Song of the Glacier drew her grandson aside. "Before you go, tell me, Audun, is something bothering you?"

"Yes, there is," Audun replied. "It was something Grandfather said. He isn't sure that you're happy to have him here."

Song of the Glacier sighed. "I suppose that's because I'm not sure myself. You know I love your grandfather, but in the time I've been a counselor to Stormclaw, the king and I have grown closer. I told you once that before old King Bent Tooth declared that I had to marry your grandfather, I knew that my true love was Stormclaw. Although I came to love your grandfather, my love for Stormclaw never changed. Now I'm torn, loving two dragons and not knowing what to do."

"When you and the king were talking in the audience chamber, I thought you two sounded like an old married couple," said Audun.

"I know," said his grandmother. "I'm as comfortable with him as I am with your grandfather, except when they're both in the castle. Ah, well, it's my problem and I'll have to deal with it. Look, your friends are waiting for you. The map is in that drawer." The old dragoness pointed to a table at the side of the room.

While Audun found the map, his grandmother took a small cloth bag out of a chest and handed it to Millie. "Here are some coins. Buy Annie and Liam any cards they want. The cards will be a wedding gift from the dragons. If you have any money left over, buy some for me as well. I want to see how they work. See if you can find one for Upper Montevista. I really would like to visit Frazzie again. By the time you get to be my age, many of your friends have moved away or died off. You should cherish the few you have left."

"I'll see if I can find some for Greater Greensward, too," said Millie. "And there might be others that you'd like."

"All set," said Audun. He had already spread the small tapestry on the table where Annie and Liam could examine it. "All we have to do is touch the wall surrounding the fountain. See, it's in the middle of the marketplace. When we get there, you'll see that the fountain is on a raised platform. We'll be able to see the entire marketplace from there."

"Including the postcard stand," Annie said, crossing her fingers.

"I hope so," said Liam. "We've been wearing the same clothes since we left home, and this shirt really itches! When we get home, the first thing I'm going to do is—"

"Is everyone ready?" Audun asked. "Put your finger on the wall when I count to three. Just think about how much you want to go there. One, two—"

"Wait!" cried Millie. "You forgot again!" She glanced down at herself, then looked pointedly at Audun.

"What?" he asked, obviously confused.

"We're dragons! We can't go there like this!"

"Oh, right," said Audun. "We'll change at the same time."

"We usually do. Ready, set . . ."

The air shimmered around both dragons, and a moment later two humans stood in their places.

Although Annie had liked Millie as a dragon, she liked her even more as a human.

"All right, let's try this again," said Audun. "One, two, three!"

The wall in the picture was made of thread, just like the rest of the tapestry. Annie was surprised when it felt cold and hard to the touch as if it really were made of stone. She blinked at a puff of air, and when she opened her eyes again, she was standing in the center of a busy marketplace with her friends by her side. They all drew their hands back from the wall at the same time and turned to look around.

The noise in the market was a little overwhelming at first. Merchants shouted, dogs barked, customers called to one another, singing swords sang while metal clanged on metal at the stall where people were trying out armor, meat sizzled on a nearby grill, and magic wind chimes rang, stirring up a breeze. Annie took a deep breath, trying to decide what smelled the best as the breeze wafted different scents toward her. Was it the meat that a cat was using tongs to turn, or the enormous flowers that nearly hid the stand displaying them? The savory meat pies were enough to make Annie's mouth water, but the delicate pastries that were so light they floated above the table almost made her forget why she was there.

"Anyone see the postcard stand?" asked Audun.

"That might be it over there," Azuria said, pointing in a direction Annie hadn't even looked at yet.

She spotted it then, a stand with tall racks placed back to back on each of the tables. Customers flocked around the racks, picking and choosing among the assorted postcards. A witch with pale green hair collected payment, while four dogs kept watch for shoplifters.

"Follow me," said Audun as he stepped off the raised platform.

Liam took Annie's hand and together they walked through the crowds, amazed by all the strange and exotic goods for sale. Annie found one stall displaying enormous seeds like the giants could have used to grow their vegetables. Intrigued, she took a step closer and almost tripped on a rabbit wearing an oversize vest.

"Want to buy a sundial, lady?" the rabbit said, opening his vest to display sewn-in straps holding miniature sundials that seemed to provide their own light.

"Hey you, no unlicensed peddlers in the marketplace!" shouted the vendor selling the giant seeds.

The rabbit looked furtive as he closed his vest and hopped away, but Annie saw him stop another customer when the seed-selling man was no longer watching.

"This is it, all right!" Azuria called to them as they reached the stall she had spotted. "Look at all these postcards. I might have to do some traveling and visit a few of these places. Look, here's one that shows a ship-wreck underwater."

"Trust me, you don't want to go there," said Liam. "You'll end up at the bottom of the ocean if you do."

A number of the people examining the cards must have heard him, because suddenly there was a rush toward the very card Liam was warning them about. Before he could ask what was happening, all of the cards showing Nastia Nautica's ship were gone.

"Why do you suppose they wanted that card?" Annie whispered to Liam. "That's the last place I'd want to go."

"Who knows?" Liam whispered back. "The people here are very odd. Just don't say anything about a card you want, or all the copies might be gone before you get there. You go that way and I'll go this way. If the cards we want are here, we'll find them faster if we split up."

Although Annie and Liam went in different direc-tions, Millie and Audun stayed together as they wan-dered around the tables, examining the cards. Azuria drifted away to talk to some women who were waving at her.

Annie made her way through the people studying the postcards. Some of them were dressed in clothes that marked them as magic users, with weird sym-bols on their sleeves or bits of magic on their hats or gowns that shot sparks or showed things like moving clouds or crashing waves. Others had a creepy aura about them that made her uncomfortable. Only a small percentage of the people looked normal. Liam was right—most of the customers in the marketplace were very odd.

When Annie finally began examining the cards, she was so excited that her hands shook. It was up to her and Liam to find the cards they needed. Although their friends wanted to help, only Annie and Liam knew what Treecrest and Dorinocco looked like.

It didn't take long for Annie to see that the postcards were separated by categories. All the cards showing castles in pretty, pastoral settings were on one long table. Pictures of mountains were on one side of a second table; deserts were on the other side. A third table held cards with pictures from everywhere else. Annie saw villages with quaint cottages made of straw and twigs, and towns where the buildings were all made of stone. She saw rolling hills and grassy plains, forests of evergreens and solitary trees on lonely hillsides. There were only a few showing islands. Annie picked out some cards that she thought might be useful, but she didn't see either Treecrest or Dorinocco.

After figuring out where the different cards were located, Annie returned to the postcards showing pictures of castles. Unfortunately, there were lots of them. There were cards showing castles of every description, from low buildings that looked as if they had been made for dwarves, to some that towered high above the trees around them. Annie had never imagined that there were so many kinds of castles!

She had been searching through the cards for a few minutes when she came across a sign stating:

Notice: This is a magic buffer zone. Postcards will not work within this zone. To use your card, stand on the fountain platform.

When she looked around, she saw that this same notice had been posted on every table.

As one person after another pushed past her, Annie searched through all the castle postcards twice, but still was unable to find one for Treecrest or Dorinocco. She found some empty slots, but none of them were labeled. Dejected, she looked for Liam.

"They don't have any for Treecrest or Dorinocco," she told him, so upset that she was close to tears. "I was so sure they'd have them. Now I don't know what we're going to do. Liam, I really want to go home, but what if we can never find it again?"

"Don't worry," Liam told her. "We'll get home somehow, even if we have to go to Nasheen's kingdom and work our way home from there."

"If we must," said Annie, "but I was hoping we'd never go to Viramoot again."

Liam shrugged. "I suppose we could go to Delaroo Pass and head home next winter if the weather isn't too bad."

"And in the meantime, everyone we love will think we're lost or dead!"

"Is something wrong?" Millie asked as she joined them.

"We can't find cards for Treecrest or Dorinocco. I don't know how we'll ever get home," Annie said with a catch in her voice.

"You could always come to Greater Greensward. I'd love to have you live close by," said Millie.

They all turned when a commotion started at the table where the witch with pale green hair was collecting money.

"What do you mean I can't get them all?" an old woman yelled at the witch. "My money is as good as anyone's!"

"Yes, but you have enough for only four cards," the witch said, obviously trying to remain patient. "You'll have to pick out the cards you want the most."

The old woman opened her mouth to yell again, closing it with a snap when two of the owner's dogs stalked to her side and began to growl.

"I guess I could get four now and come back later with more money," grumbled the elderly woman.

"Here, I'll take these." Snatching the top four from the pile, she stomped off, muttering to herself.

The green-haired witch sighed and shook her head as she picked up the remaining cards. While the dogs guarded the money box, she walked down the tables, returning the unpurchased cards to their slots. When Annie saw her head to the table with the castle post-cards, she hurried over to study each card as it was replaced. Other customers were hovering around the witch as well, curious about what she was putting back. A wizard in a tall peaked hat was reaching for a card when Annie realized that it showed the castle in Treecrest. With a horrified gasp, she stepped in front of the table and grabbed all the cards picturing Treecrest, knocking his hand out of the way.

"Pardon me!" he said, glaring down his long, pointy nose at her.

"Sorry!" Annie called as she turned and ran back to Liam and her friends while clutching the card to her chest.

"Did you get it?" asked Liam, taking the cards from her. "There are three here. Why would that old woman need all three?"

"Do you want to put some back?" asked Millie. "That man really seemed to want one, too. Look, he's coming this way."

"Please don't tell him there were three," said Annie. "I already have plans for all of them. Besides, did you look at that man? I really don't think my parents want him to drop by."

Azuria had returned from talking to her friends. "That's the wizard Bromley," she said. "My sister used to date his brother. You're absolutely right. He would make a terrible house guest. I hear he bathes once every ten years, whether he needs it or not."

The wizard stomped up and glared at Annie. "That was very rude, young lady! By all rights, that card should be mine. Give it to me now or you'll regret you ever came here."

"I'm sorry, sir, but I can't give it to you," said Annie. "That card is a picture of my home and I've been looking for a way to get back."

"Bromley!" said Azuria. "It's been years. Remember me? I'm Azuria. Your brother, Grimwold, used to date my sister, Dorelle. If they had gotten married, you and I would be almost-relatives now. Maybe I can help you. You wanted a picture of a nice castle? I'm sure we can find another one. Why don't I help you look?"

"I don't remember you," said the wizard.

"Of course you do," Azuria said, taking his arm and hustling him away. "I'm ten years younger than Dorelle and was always underfoot. I remember one day when you came looking for Grimwold and you had a sack of weasels with you. Why, I . . ."

"He did look angry," said Annie as she watched Azuria lead the wizard to the postcards. "I wonder why he wanted a postcard for Treecrest so badly."

"I heard some people talking," Millie told her. "I think they're competing to see who can visit the most out-of-the-way places."

"Did you get what you were looking for?" Audun asked as he rejoined the group. "I found quite a few interesting cards myself."

Annie smiled. "We got what we needed. Now we can go home!"

"If you're finished looking, I'll go pay for the cards. Here, give them all to me," said Millie.

While Millie and Audun went to pay for the post-cards, Liam turned to Annie. "I'm as anxious to get home as you are," he told her, "but do you mind if we stay here a little longer? There's something I really want to look at and I won't be but a minute."

"I suppose we could," Annie told him. He looked as eager and excited as a small boy expecting a big treat, and she didn't want be the one to disappoint him. "What did you want to look at?"

"There's a stall over that way," he said, pointing. "I saw it from the fountain platform. I just hope there isn't a big crowd."

"Audun and I will go with you," Millie said, returning with her purchases in her hand. "The marketplace is so much fun! I love seeing all the new things they have for sale."

"Here's Azuria," said Annie. "What happened with Bromley?"

"Don't worry about him," the old witch replied. "I found him some other postcards he'd never seen before. He seems quite happy now. Apparently, he's competing in a contest with other wizards. It's just as well you took all three postcards, Annie. I have a feeling that those wizards are up to no good. You really don't want them to visit Treecrest! If you'll excuse me, I'm going to say good-bye now. My friends invited me to dinner. Thank you for your help, everyone! Annie, Liam, I'm sure I'll see you again someday. Millie, I'll see you in a few days. Your mother has asked me to help her plan the next meeting of the witches' council. She's letting them hold it at your castle."

"What do you find so interesting, Liam?" Annie asked as she followed him to another stall.

"Singing swords!" he said, and began to run ahead.

"My father has a singing sword," said Millie. "Its name is Ferdy."

"Huh," grunted Audun. "That sword doesn't like me."

"Do the swords have personalities?" Annie asked.

"Ferdy does," said Millie. "He doesn't like to fight, but he does it when my father needs him to."

"Stupid sword," grumbled Audun.

Millie and Audun joined Annie at the end of the singing sword stall with their backs to the stall where a man was selling wind chimes. Liam hurried to the swords displayed on the table and picked up one etched with a gold-and-silver design. The stall owner was talking to another customer, but he smiled and nodded at Liam.

"Do you smell that?" one well-dressed wizard asked, sniffing in Annie's direction.

Annie blushed. She hadn't bathed in days, and her clothes were a little stained and dirty, but she didn't think she was *that* bad. After all, she had gone swimming with Liam at the giants' island, and that wasn't that long ago.

"I don't like swords myself," Audun said in a quiet voice. "Dragons don't need them, and when I'm human, I'd rather turn into a dragon if I have to fight."

"Most people don't have that ability," Millie reminded him. "A singing sword could be very useful."

"What do you think of this one?" Liam called to Annie. When he held up the sword, it began to sing in a slightly off-key voice.

Pick me up and try me out,
You'll see that I am great!

"Do you really need a singing sword?" Annie asked Liam.

"Who doesn't? I've heard about them, but I never thought I could own one. Here, look at the etching on the blade. It's perfect!"

The sword was still singing when Liam carried it to show Annie, Millie, and Audun.

Raise me high and swing me hard,
I am a perfect weight.

"I really don't think . . . ," Annie began.

As soon as it was close to Annie, the sword's song began to falter. After a few words, it stopped singing altogether.

Liam began to frown. "Maybe this isn't such a good idea."

A few other customers had stopped by to examine swords. One by one, the voices of the other swords failed, starting with the ones closest to Annie. The breeze that had been wafting through the marketplace died down as the wind chimes at the next stall grew silent.

"What's happening?" asked the man who was selling singing swords. "How can this be?"

The man selling wind chimes was becoming frantic, running from one to the next, poking some and giving others a good shake.

"We need to go," Annie told Liam.

"Does anyone smell that?" said a man who had been passing behind Annie and her friends. "I swear that smells like dragon. Is anyone selling dragon parts here?"

"Did you hear that? Someone is selling dragon parts!" cried another passerby.

The rumor spread throughout the market, creating even more excitement than Annie had seen at the post-card stand. She glanced at Millie and Audun. Although she had grown used to the way they smelled and didn't really notice it that much anymore, she could understand how it might attract attention.

"We need to go, too," Audun said, ushering Millie toward the fountain. People were running through the marketplace, searching for the source of the smell, but it didn't seem to occur to anyone that the smell might be coming from living, breathing dragons.

Annie and Liam hurried after their friends, although Annie did notice that Liam cast a wistful glance at the sword he had left on the table.

"We forgot to put on the lotion that covers up our dragon smell," Audun told the others when they reached the raised platform. "We don't need it in Greater Greensward or the ice-dragon stronghold, so we don't use it very often."

"Why are those people so excited about dragon parts?" asked Annie. "People don't actually buy them, do they?"

Audun was scowling when he said, "They would if they could get their hands on them."

"Even a tiny piece of a dragon has strong magic," explained Millie. "If someone can include it in a spell, his magic would be that much more powerful."

"That's gruesome!" said Annie.

Millie shrugged. "Magic users don't get dragon parts very often. Usually they become available if someone comes across a dragon that died alone in some isolated spot.

"And on that note, I think we should go before those people notice that the smell is stronger up here," said Millie, gesturing to the people still sniffing the air. "Here are the Treecrest postcards." She opened the sack from the postcard vendor and reached inside. "And the others that you picked out. I've also included a few we thought you'd like. You already have a card for Greater Greensward, but I included one for Upper Montevista, where my father's parents live. We'd like you to come visit us in Greater Greensward when you can."

"And we'd like you to visit us," Annie told them, handing a card back. "I wanted one of the Treecrest cards for you. I grew up there and my parents live there still. If I'd found some for Dorinocco, I'd give you one of those as well. Liam is going to be crowned king of Dorinocco when we get back."

"How exciting!" said Millie. "Then you'll probably be very busy for some time to come."

"I'm sure we will." When Annie saw Millie's disappointed expression, she added, "But we'll never be too busy for friends."

"The sign said that the postcards would work up here," said Liam. "Are you ready, Annie?" He held out the card for Treecrest with one finger poised above it.

"Just a moment," she told him before turning to Millie and Audun. "I want to say thank you. We might never have been able to go home again if you hadn't helped us."

"You're very welcome!" said Millie. "It was fun!"

"Here," Annie said, digging into her pocket. She took out the fur doll that the yeti Mara had given to her and handed it to Millie. "I want you to have this for your baby. A very nice yeti gave it to me."

"What baby?" Millie asked, looking confused.

"The one you're going to have, of course," said Annie. "You know I can hear magic, right? Apparently I can hear dragon magic, too, whether you're in your dragon or human form. I guess that's because dragons don't just have magic, you *are* magic, which is probably why your magic is so powerful. Anyway, when I first met you I noticed that dragon magic sounds like music. Yours has a simple countermelody running through it. I thought that was just your individual magic, but then I met all those other dragons at the stronghold and none of them had that. Your second melody seems to get stronger each day, so I figured it wasn't yours at all. It was your baby's. Congratulations!"

Millie and Audun didn't say anything. They had turned to each other in a daze, but even now delight was dawning in their eyes.

"I guess they didn't know," Annie told Liam.

"We need to go," he reminded her, and showed her the postcard again.

Annie was about to say good-bye to her new friends, but from the way they were gazing at each other, she doubted they would hear her. Smiling to herself, she reached for the postcard. A moment later, Annie and Liam vanished.

CHAPTER 17

"I SAW LOTS of castles on those postcards, but I still think this is the most beautiful," Annie said with a sigh. "Although your father's castle is lovely, too," she hurried to add.

"It will be when we move in," said Liam. "After we talk to your parents, I want to go to Dorinocco. It's about time I set the date for my coronation."

"But what about—"

A puff of silver sparkles just a few feet from where they stood heralded Moonbeam's arrival. The little woods witch Holly was there, too, blinking and looking confused. "You're back!" Moonbeam cried, clapping her hands. "I was so worried, especially after I talked to Holly and heard how she got the postcards."

"What are you talking about?" asked Liam.

"Remember how I told you that I would take care of Rotan? Well, I would have, but I couldn't find him anywhere. I asked around and heard that the last time anyone had seen him, he was on his way to the Magic Marketplace. That made me curious, so I looked up Holly and asked her a few questions. Holly, tell them what you told me."

The little woods witch looked even more confused. "Um, I told you that I liked your sparkles?"

"No, no! The thing about Rotan. You know, the wizard you met at the Magic Marketplace?"

"Oh, right! Like I said before, I went to the Magic Marketplace to buy you a gift. I was sure I'd find something that newlyweds could use, but when I got there nothing seemed quite right. I was telling a man selling bottomless tankards why I was buying a gift and who it was for, when this very nice gentleman suggested that I get you postcards. He said that lots of young couples like to go on a trip after their wedding, and I was sure he was right. The gentleman even helped me pick them out. When I told Moonbeam that, she was very upset, but she never did tell me what I did wrong. I didn't, did I? Do something wrong, I mean."

Liam shook his head. "The only thing you did wrong was to trust a stranger, but no one can really fault you for that."

"Then I can go now?" asked Holly. "Moonbeam said I had to stay until you came back, but some of my plants are ready for picking and I have to collect them at just the right time."

"You may go," said Annie. A moment later, Holly disappeared, leaving only drifting leaves and the scent of pine behind.

"So, did you run into Rotan?" asked Moonbeam. "What did he do?"

"Apparently he picked out cards that presented their own unique difficulties," said Liam. "Then he visited each location to tell people lies about us. He certainly didn't make our tour any easier."

"I'm just glad you're back safe and sound," said Moonbeam. "I must go tell your parents. They've been so worried about you."

"You know," Annie said to Liam as Moonbeam hurried off, "looking back on it, our grand tour wasn't too terrible. I might actually have enjoyed parts of it if I hadn't been so worried that we might never get home."

"I knew we would eventually," Liam said.

Annie coughed, trying to choke down laughter. She was certain that Liam had been just as worried, but she doubted that he'd ever admit it now.

They had started toward the castle, hand in hand, when Annie remembered what they had been discussing when Moonbeam had arrived. "You were telling me that you're ready to be crowned," she reminded Liam. "What about your mother and Clarence? Have you decided what you want to do about them?"

"I have," said Liam. "Our trip inspired me. I think it's time both my mother and Clarence went to live somewhere far away. Separately, of course. They always get into trouble when they're together."

"In that case, I think our trip was very successful," Annie said, giving Liam's hand a squeeze. "You've decided what you'll do with your mother and brother, we made some new friends, and we took care of Rotan so he won't bother us anymore."

"There was one more thing," said Liam. "I wanted to take you to places you had never visited before, places where you could see new and unusual things and meet different kinds of people. That's exactly what we ended up doing. As far as I'm concerned, we had the best grand tour ever!"

The magic continues in the Wide-Awake Princess series!

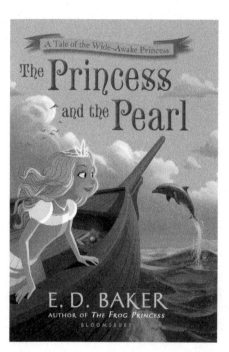

When Princess Annie's father falls ill and no doctors in Treecrest can cure him, there's only one person who might be able to help—a healer who lives in Skull Cove. To journey there, Annie must set sail on dangerous seas, where she finds out that the only cure for her father is a giant pearl held captive by a sea witch. Can Annie find the pearl before it's too late?

Princess Annie stepped into her chamber and glanced at all the trunks that servants had packed in her absence, preparing for her move to Dorinocco. Liam was about to be crowned king, which meant that Annie would always want to look her best. She was taking her nicer gowns and would have more made upon her arrival. She already knew that she would miss Treecrest, but the two kingdoms were close enough that she planned to visit often.

Annie had slipped off her shoes and was placing them by her bed when a disembodied head appeared in the corner. "Where have you been?" the face asked, scowling. Startled, it took Annie a moment to remember that the magic mirror was in that corner now.

"You left me all alone for days without telling me where you were going or when I'd see you again!" the face declared. "Why would you do that?"

"I'm sorry," Annie replied. "Liam and I didn't expect to leave when we did. I couldn't have told you where we were going because we didn't know until we got there. It wasn't an ordinary grand tour."

"You went on your grand tour!" said the face in the mirror. "No one told me that! All those ladies came to consult me about their love lives, and not one of them told me a thing!"

"So you weren't all alone!" said Annie. "Who came to see you?"

"Just a few people. Your sister came first, then Lady Patrice and Lady Cecily and Lady Clare and Lady Josephine and Lady Hortense and three kitchen maids named Ula, Bev, and Winnie. You wouldn't believe what they asked me!"

"I'm not interested in gossip," said Annie.

The face in the mirror looked outraged. "This isn't gossip! I'm just telling you about my conversations."

Annie turned away when she heard a knock on the door, opening it to admit servants carrying buckets of steaming water. She had worn the same clothes for the entire trip. They were so filthy now that she didn't want to sit on her bed or chair, so she waited while the servants filled the tub and set the screen in front of the magic mirror so he couldn't see past it. The face in the mirror grumbled, but Annie didn't care. All she could think about now was a nice hot bath and finally getting clean.

The moment the door closed, Annie disrobed and stepped into the tub. Although the water felt too hot at first, she eased her way in and sat back, letting the warmth relax her tired muscles. Within minutes, Annie felt better than she had in days. True, she had enjoyed a bath in the palace in Westerling, and gone swimming at the giants' island, but she hadn't felt truly safe and able to fully unwind until now.

Annie and Liam had been planning to sail along the coastline for their grand tour, but news of an evil wizard and the gift of magic postcards from a woods witch had sent them on an unexpected trip. If their lives hadn't been in danger wherever they went, they might have enjoyed it more, but they had visited places they hadn't known existed and made new and highly unusual friends. They had even visited Annie's uncle, Rupert, someone she had never met before. The grand tour had been shorter than she and Liam had planned, and not at all where they'd wanted to go, but it had been marvelous and exciting.

Annie glanced out the window. It was getting late in the day; she'd have to dress for supper in a little while. She had wanted to see her parents as soon as she got back, but they had been in a meeting and unable to see her then. Although she'd wondered what kind of meeting would have kept them from welcoming her and Liam, she was glad to have a chance to get cleaned up first. Liam had been eager to bathe as well, and had gone to the room he'd used before the wedding, hoping his clothes were still there.

Annie dozed until the water cooled enough to fully wake her. She washed then, scrubbing her skin and hair until the last vestiges of her trip were gone. After drying off, she put on an old peach-colored gown that wasn't good enough to pack, brushed her hair, and started for the door.

"Leaving without saying good-bye again?" said the face in the mirror.

"I'm just going to supper," Annie replied. "I'll be back soon."

"Just don't go on any long trips without telling me first," said the mirror.

Annie took a step back into the room. She hadn't been planning to take the magic mirror with her when she moved to Dorinocco, but maybe it wouldn't be a bad idea. The face in the mirror had been useful at times and she had almost started to like it. "Liam and I are going to Dorinocco," she said. "His father is stepping down and Liam is going to be crowned king. We'll be living there from now on. Would you like to come with us?"

"You were leaving without me? I knew something was going on when people packed up all your clothes! Of course I want to come! You may like tapestries of unicorns and flowers way too much and your singing makes me wish I could plug my ears, but being with you is a lot better than being with Queen Marissa. She was almost as horrible to me as she was to Snow White. That woman gave me no respect! I don't know how many times she threatened to toss me into the moat or a pit full of snakes. I hate snakes! They squiggle through the muck and leave ugly trails all over your nice, clean glass."

"Then you're welcome to come," said Annie. "I'll let the steward know that you need to be loaded on the cart before we leave." She had started out the door again when something occurred to her. Once again, she turned back to face the mirror. "I don't understand something. You can see what other people are doing all the time. When I was gone, why didn't you just look for me?"

"I tried," said the mirror. "But I could never find you. Magic doesn't work on you, remember?"

"I didn't realize it would block you from seeing me," Annie said. "I learn something new every day. I'll try to remember to tell you whenever I'm going away, if that will make you happy."

"Delirious," said the face, although it still looked grumpy.

On her way down the stairs, Annie thought about what the mirror had said. It hadn't occurred to her that the mirror couldn't see her when she was away, but then it wasn't really a surprise. Since the day the fairy Moonbeam gave Annie her one and only magical christening gift, she had been impervious to magic. Not only would magic bounce off Annie if someone tried to cast a spell on her, but everyone else's magic faded when she was nearby. Annie had thought this would always be true, and it wasn't until she received the magic postcards that she learned there was a form of magic stronger than the fairy kind. Dragon magic was the strongest of all. It was the one kind of magic that affected Annie as much as it did everyone else. It was the reason she and Liam had been able to use the magic postcards. It was also the reason they'd been able to come back home.

Annie was halfway down the stairs when people started to greet her. The entire time she was growing up, she'd been shunned by relatives, courtiers, and anyone made more attractive or talented through magic. After she broke her sister's curse, her family had warmed to her and the others hadn't avoided her quite as much. However, since the day of her wedding, these same courtiers seemed to be drawn to her. Not only had she brought the fairies to repair the damage to the castle, making up for the spells they had cast, but she had ended King Dormander's siege as well. What people seemed to remember the most, however, was the wedding the fairies had put on for her. They were still talking about it as they stopped her on the stairway.

"It was the most beautiful thing I've ever seen," one elderly courtier said, surprising Annie because the woman had never spoken to her before.

"I cried during your wedding, and I never cry! Not even when my dear Randolf died!" said another older woman.

"I still cry every time I think about it!" a third woman told her.

Unsure how to respond, Annie smiled and nodded and hurried down the stairs. The fairies had outdone themselves and it had been a beautiful wedding, but so many other things had happened since then that Annie felt as if the wedding had taken place long ago.

When Annie reached the great hall, it was as crowded and noisy as usual. Ewan, the young redheaded page, met her at the door. "Her Highness Queen Karolina asks that you sit at the high table from now on," he said. "This way, if you please."

Annie smiled after he turned away. The boy was so proud of his position and excited about what he was doing that she almost had to laugh. When she glanced at the dais, where her parents usually sat, she saw Liam waiting for her. Her parents weren't there, but she expected to see them any minute.

"Are Princess Gwendolyn and Prince Beldegard still in the castle?" she asked Ewan.

The page shook his head. "They left for Montrose two days ago. No one expects them back anytime soon."

Liam stood as Annie approached the dais. "You look ... clean!" she said with a smile.

Liam laughed. "So do you! I feel much better now. It's amazing what a hot bath and clean clothes can do for a person. Now all I need is to sleep for about three days and I'll be back to normal."

"That sounds tempting," said Annie. "When did you want to go to Dorinocco?"

Liam pushed her seat in for her, then sat down, saying, "I suppose we should go as soon as possible. We have a lot to do if I'm to take over from my father. If we get a good night's rest tonight, we can leave early tomorrow morning."

"We still have to decide where we're going to send Clarence and your mother," said Annie.

"I know," Liam said, frowning. "The sooner we do that, the better."

Liam's mother, Queen Lenore, and his brother, Prince Clarence, had conspired to take over Annie's home kingdom of Treecrest. When the tiny spinning wheel they'd sent had made Gwennie's curse come true, Annie had found princes to wake her sister with a kiss. King Montague had locked his queen in a tower, but Clarence had run off to sea, returning with a nasty wizard who assisted in the siege of King Halbert's castle. Both Clarence and Queen Lenore were locked in King Montague's castle now, but Liam didn't want them anywhere nearby when he became king.

"Your Highness," said a voice at Annie's side. She turned to find Ewan waiting by her elbow. "Your mother,

Queen Karolina, has sent word that she and King Halbert will not be joining you for supper tonight. She asks that you come to the king's chamber after you've eaten."

"In that case, please tell the servers that they may begin," Annie told the page. No one ate before the king and queen arrived, but if they weren't coming...

Although the salmon was delicious, Annie couldn't do more than pick at her food. Something was wrong, she could feel it. Why else had her parents been unable to see her when she returned home? And why weren't they coming down to supper?

Seeing her unease, Liam ate quickly and they were soon headed upstairs to her father's chamber. Her mother met them at the door, ushering them to the chair where King Halbert was waiting. Annie had rarely seen him in his nightclothes before. Finding him dressed in a long robe and slippers made her worry even more. "What's wrong?" Annie asked as soon as she saw him. "Did something happen?"

"Your father isn't feeling well," said the queen. "It started last night. We had the doctor come see him today, but the man was worthless. He said he'd never seen anything like it before."

"Like what?" asked Annie. King Halbert sighed. "Your mother is making a big fuss over nothing. It's just a touch of stomach sickness, that's all. I wasn't able to eat last night or today, but I should be fine by tomorrow."

"That is not all it is and you know it!" declared the queen. "Show her your feet!"

"I'm not showing anyone my feet!" said the king.

"She's your daughter. She has the right to know what's going on!" the queen told him. "Show her your feet, Halbert, or I'll do it for you!"

King Halbert glared at his wife. When she glared back, he sighed and pulled his feet out of his slippers. Annie gasped. Her father's feet were blue. Not the kind of blue her feet turned when she'd been swimming in cold water too long, but the bright blue of a gown her mother often wore.

"Do they hurt?" she asked her father, kneeling down beside him.

"Not at all!" said the king. "They feel perfectly normal; they just look like I've been stomping blue grapes to make wine. I'm sure the color doesn't mean a thing. As soon as I get over this stomach sickness, I'll be up and around again."

Annie turned to her mother. "Can you send for another doctor?"

"No!" declared King Halbert. "They're all quacks! I don't want another of those blustering idiots near me! I'm fine, I tell you. I didn't have you come up here to fuss over me like your mother. I just want to hear about your trip. Moonbeam told us that you went by postcard. What an interesting way to travel! Pull up some chairs and tell me all about it. You might as well sit down, too,

Karolina. I know you're just as curious as I am, and I don't want you hovering over me any more tonight."

"Are you sure I can't send for anything for you?" said the queen.

"I'm positive," said the king. "Annie, start at the beginning. I want to hear everything!"

THE NEXT MORNING, Annie and Liam woke as the sun came up, hoping to get an early start. After a quick breakfast of bread hot from the oven spread with butter and soft cheese, they went upstairs to see her parents. Annie's father was still in bed, but she was pleased to see that he was awake and looked better than he had the night before.

"How are you feeling, Father?" asked Annie.

"Much better," said the king. "Your mother gave me a tonic to help me sleep last night. My stomach isn't bothering me nearly as much today. I've already sent for breakfast, so there's no need to worry about me."

"If you're all right, Liam and I will be leaving this morning," Annie told him.

"I expected as much," her father told her. "Have a safe trip and come back for a visit as soon as you can."

Annie and Liam went to say good-bye to the queen

next. She had gone for an early-morning walk in the garden with some of her ladies-in-waiting. Although Queen Karolina had dark circles under her eyes, she assured Annie that everything was all right. "You're about to start a whole new life with your husband," said the queen. "I don't want you to worry about your father and me. We'll be fine. I'm sure your father was right. It was just a temporary indisposition. He'll be up and about today."

"If you're sure . . . ," said Annie.

"I am," said the queen. "I know King Montague is looking forward to your arrival. Don't keep Liam's father waiting any longer than you must."

Once the queen had dismissed them, Annie and Liam hurried to the courtyard, anxious to get started. Annie had sent money to pay for Otis and was looking forward to riding the gelding that day. With Liam riding Hunter, it felt almost like the trip they had taken from Dorinocco to the Garden of Happiness, only this time no one was chasing them, thankfully. They also had an escort of half a dozen knights to guard them, along with another half-dozen men guarding the wagon hauling Annie's belongings.

The magic mirror had been crammed into the wagon at the last minute, and Annie could still hear it grumbling as they crossed over the drawbridge. "Does the driver have to aim for every bump and pothole!" it called out.

"Let's ride ahead a bit," Annie said to Liam. "I really

don't want to hear the magic mirror complaining the whole way there. If I'd known it was going to be like that, I would have left it in my old bedroom."

"I heard that!" shouted the mirror.

Annie sighed and urged Otis to go a little faster. When the two horses trotted ahead, the six knights hurried to catch up, leaving half the group behind. Annie and Liam were still in the lead when they came to a crossroad where an elderly woman was sitting on a large rock.

Annie groaned and said, "Not that witch again! She must live close by. I see her every time I come this way."

"There you are!" the old woman shouted. A lizard slipped out of her mouth and a frog fell to the ground in a shower of rose petals. "Do you know how long I've been waiting for you? It's your fault I'm in this mess!" Spewing pearls like a messy eater dribbles crumbs, she made a horrible face when a snake slithered between her lips and tumbled to her lap.

"I didn't do anything to you," said Annie. "You wouldn't be in this mess if you didn't keep trying to cast spells on me."

"Whatever! It's going to end today," said the woman, and gagged on a pair of squirming salamanders. After wiping a rose petal off her tongue, she added, "I found a reversal spell that has got to work!"

The woman called out while waving her hands in the

air. Her words were garbled as toads, frogs, and a long, skinny snake with an arrow-shaped head slithered out of her mouth. A gray-green cloud swept toward Annie, roiled around in front of her, and washed back over the old witch.

"That should do it!" the witch declared.

When nothing squiggled from between her lips or fell from her mouth, she hopped up and down, clapping her hands in delight. Weeds near her feet began to rustle, but she didn't seem to notice.

"It worked!" she shouted. A big, warty toad emerged from the weeds. In one bound, it leaped at the witch, hitting her in the mouth. If her mouth hadn't been closed, the toad might have gone inside. Instead, it hit her lips and fell to the ground, landing on its back.

"What was that?" the witch cried. Rose petals that had fallen from her mouth just minutes before flew at her, pressing themselves to her lips.

Annie and Liam were almost past when the old woman screamed, "No!"

As pearls hurtled toward her face and a snake slithered onto her foot, the old woman clasped her hands over her mouth and ran into the forest.

"Let me guess," said Liam. "The old woman's reversal spell worked a little too well. No weird things are coming out of her mouth now. Instead, they're all trying to go back in!"

Annie nodded. "I think you're right. You know, if I were her, I'd become a hermit and never speak to anyone again!"

They could hear the wagon carrying Annie's possessions coming up behind them when they turned onto the road leading to Farley's Crossing. The small town had grown up around the only ferry that crossed the Crystal River and was a common destination for travelers. It took Annie and Liam's group more than an hour to get there. When they arrived, the ferry was loading and already nearly full. One of the knights rode up to tell the ferryman that the prince and princess wanted to cross and the surly man's eyes lit up.

"Do they now?" he said. He thought for a moment and named a price higher than anyone else would have to pay. When the guard nodded, the man chortled and turned to the passengers already on board. "You have to get off and wait for the next crossing!" he shouted at them.

The passengers got off without complaint, moving aside to let the new arrivals on while eyeing them with interest.

"This trip is so different from any we've ever taken together," Annie told Liam as they rode onto the ferry. "That was nice of the ferryman to let us get on now, and even nicer of all those people to get off for us."

"The ferryman did it because he knew he could get more money from us," said Liam. "The people did it because he was making them get off, plus they could watch us until the ferry leaves. Most of them have never seen a royal party before."

"Either way, it was nice of them," said Annie. "People don't usually treat me with that much respect."

"They will from now on," Liam said, his expression turning serious. "You're about to be Queen Annabelle of Dorinocco!"

"Have you decided what you want to do with Clarence and your mother?" asked Annie.

"I haven't decided where to take my mother, but I know what I want to do with Clarence. How do you think your uncle Rupert would feel about a permanent guest?"

"He might actually like it. They never have guests at the fortress and it would be someone for him to talk to other than his own soldiers."

"And Clarence wouldn't be able to get into much mischief," said Liam. "I think that's where we'll take him. We'll go first thing tomorrow. The sooner we get Clarence and my mother out of the castle, the happier I'll be."

E. D. BAKER is the author of the Tales of the Frog Princess series, the Wide-Awake Princess series, the Fairy-Tale Matchmaker series, and many other delightful books for young readers, including *A Question of Magic, Fairy Wings*, and *Fairy Lies*. Her first book, *The Frog Princess*, was the inspiration for Disney's hit movie *The Princess and the Frog*. She lives with her family and their many animals in Maryland.

www.talesofedbaker.com

Enter the magical world of
E. D. Baker!

Read the entire
Frog Princess
series!